THE EMPEROR EXPECTS

THE BEAST ARISES

Book 1 – I AM SLAUGHTER
Dan Abnett

Book 2 – PREDATOR, PREY
Rob Sanders

Book 3 – THE EMPEROR EXPECTS
Gav Thorpe

Book 4 – THE LAST WALL
David Annandale

Discover the latest books in this multi-volume series at
blacklibrary.com

THE BEAST ARISES

BOOK THREE

THE EMPEROR EXPECTS

GAV THORPE

BLACK LIBRARY

This book is dedicated to the memory of Dudley Pope and C. S. Forester;
their creations had a profound influence on my adolescent mind.

A BLACK LIBRARY PUBLICATION

First published in Great Britain in 2016 by
Black Library
Games Workshop Ltd
Willow Road
Nottingham NG7 2WS UK

10 9 8 7 6 5 4 3 2 1

Produced by Games Workshop in Nottingham

A CIP record for this book is available from the British Library.

UK ISBN 13: 978 1 78496 126 8
US ISBN 13: 978 1 78496 189 3

See Black Library on the internet at
blacklibrary.com

Find out more about Games Workshop
and the world of Warhammer 40,000 at
games-workshop.com

Printed and bound in China

Fire sputters…
The shame of our deaths
and our heresies is done. They are
behind us, like wretched phantoms. This
is a new age, a strong age, an age of Imperium.
Despite our losses, despite the fallen sons, despite the
eternal silence of the Emperor, now watching over us in
spirit instead of in person, we will endure. There will be no
more war on such a perilous scale. There will be an end
to wanton destruction. Yes, foes will come and
enemies will arise. Our security will be
threatened, but we will be ready, our
mighty fists raised. There will be no
great war to challenge us now.
We will not be brought
to the brink like that
again…

Echoes of future fates...

Metamorphosis is the most powerful adaptation the universe possesses. The power of not only transformation but utter re-invention could be considered an evolutionary pinnacle. It is the ultimate change, from one state to another, triggered by pressure both internal and external.

As a response to threat, metamorphosis allows prey to become predator; endangered to become survivor; sterile consumer to become reproductive producer. With complete transformation, a step-change in inherent qualities, single organisms can continue to thrive in previously adverse conditions.

A sentient species or pan-system civilisation that is capable of metamorphosis – true metamorphosis from one state to a completely different state – is a force that can be met only with equal metamorphosis by its competitors; either the metamorphic euphemism of death or profound self-change.

Those that cannot lift themselves above their past are doomed to be swallowed by it.

ONE

Lepidus Prime – orbital, 544.M32

'*Colossus*, this is orbital command. I say again, change heading to six-three-eight, ascent forty-one. You are set on collision course with the *Noble Voyager*.'

'Ignore her,' said Captain Rafal Kulik. 'Continue on course.'

Kulik was a tall, heavy set man with a face lined by years, though a life spent in warp space made any estimate of his true age impossible. His skin was dark brown, as were his eyes, though his hair was silvery grey, its tight coils straightened and parted formally by the application of much lotion and toil every morning.

He wore his service uniform – epaulettes and cuffs of golden thread on a coat of deep blue, but no medals except for an aquila holding the badge of the Segmentum Solar, indicating Kulik's rank as a flag-captain and patrol commander. His black boots were brightly polished. A sturdy boarding cutlass was held on a hanger at his waist, with a blocky service laspistol hung at the other hip.

The atmosphere on the bridge was tense and quiet,

sparked by the mood of the man who commanded the fate of everybody aboard the battleship. Kulik dominated proceedings with his presence. He stood square in the middle of the main command deck in a serene bubble of importance – genuine authority, not self-importance – while around him junior officers waited in anticipation of his next command and half-human servitors murmured and burbled a litany of reports from the battleship's systems.

The bridge was a flattened semicircle in shape, nearly eighty feet wide with a vaulted ceiling sixty feet high; a command deck at the bottom and two mezzanine-like observation and navigation decks above. A multi-part viewing display, which could be formatted to create a variety of screens and sub-screens, dominated the chamber. It currently showed two main split-screens with a schematic of the packed orbital berths around Lepidus Prime and a scrolling list of the capital ships currently identified in the system. *Black Duke*, *Kingmaker*, *Emperor's Fortitude*, *Vigilanti Eternus*, *Fortune's Favour*, *Saviour of Delphis*, *Neptune*, *Argos*, *Uziel*: a list of forty-six and still growing.

The *Colossus* was a rare Oberon-class ship, fitted for extended solitary patrols. Her decks carried a mix of weapons batteries, high-powered lance turrets and flight bays. A dedicated tracking sensor and communications array for these systems and flight crews was manned by three officers on a sub-deck just in front of the captain's empty command throne; beyond them was set a broad secondary display dedicated to the tactical disposition of the battleship's flight assets.

With a hiss of pneumatics, the main doors to Kulik's right opened; the two armsmen sentries snapped to attention and presented their shotcannons. First Lieutenant Saul Shaffenbeck entered at a brisk pace. Shaffenbeck was prim, proper, tall and handsome like the stereotypical image of a Naval officer used by the recruiters, although somewhat in his later years now. His hair had lost none of its lustre, due to an illicit supply of dye, Kulik suspected, and though several years his captain's senior the lieutenant moved with an energy and grace that gave him the appearance of a much younger man. Shaffenbeck had never applied for his commission as captain and was the longest-serving officer on the *Colossus*. He had never explained why he was content to remain a first officer rather than a commander, but Shaffenbeck's natural calm and enviable experience made him a valuable aide; like his predecessors, Kulik was silently pleased Shaffenbeck had never sought further promotion.

The captain noticed Shaffenbeck steal a glance towards the second lieutenant at the comms panel, Mister Hartnell, as he entered. It was the briefest look before Shaffenbeck sought Kulik's permission to enter with a tilt of the head. Kulik granted permission with a nod in return. By the time Shaffenbeck was by his side Kulik had deciphered the lieutenants' exchange of glances: having failed to convince his captain to change course as requested by orbital command, the officer of the watch, Mister Hartnell, had secretly sought support from the first lieutenant.

'I do not remember requesting my first officer's presence,' said Kulik, not looking at his second-in-command but keeping his gaze on the main display.

'I was monitoring communications, sir, and happened to overhear recent exchanges with orbital command. I felt it prudent to be on hand should we require sensitive manoeuvring.'

'I'm sure that is entirely correct, lieutenant.' Kulik looked sideways at his second and gave him a glance that conveyed that the captain knew exactly what was going on and was prepared to accept this white lie to avoid imminent debate, but would possibly raise the matter at a later opportunity. In return, Shaffenbeck's slow blink and slight incline of the head transmitted equally well that he also knew exactly what was going on and was prepared to accept the consequences. Such a momentary exchange was possible only through a familiarity brought about by long years of extended, isolated patrol.

Having swiftly and silently reached this understanding, and in doing so received tacit permission to speak to his captain about the current situation, Shaffenbeck cleared his throat.

'It would seem, sir, that our current heading would bring us to an orbital berth that is presently occupied by the *Noble Voyager*.'

'I believe what you meant to say, lieutenant, is that our current destination, an orbital berth suited to a battleship commanded by a flag-captain of fifteen true-years' seniority, is currently occupied by a grand cruiser under the command of a three-year newcomer.'

'And Captain Ellis has responded to the situation how, sir?'

'He's done nothing, directly.' Kulik stiffened and looked directly at his second. 'I know you think I'm simply being obstinate, Saul, but the situation is intolerable. The whole Lepidus System is overrun with Navy ships. The fact that Admiral Acharya's fleet arrived earlier does not grant them preferential status. Orbital berths are designated by size of vessel, rank and seniority to ensure that the most important vessels and experienced commanders have better access to the supply tenders and orbital stations. Ellis must have cried to Acharya that I want him to move further out, and now the admiral is leaning on orbital. Orbital command are out of order saying that I must defer to the damned *Noble Voyager*!'

Before the lieutenant could respond a fresh broadcast blared from the bridge's speakers.

'Commander of *Colossus*, this is orbital command. By order of Admiral Acharya, you are to stand-off orbital station, assuming berth designated sigma-seven. We are re-routing the *Endeavour* to accommodate this new heading.'

'I understand completely, captain,' said Shaffenbeck, and he seemed sincere. 'However, it is hardly the fault of orbital command and your current course of action is more problematic for them than the source of your anger.'

Kulik shook his head, but his mood was already softening, the irritation he felt salved by quiet words of reason.

'The logistarius have a lot to deal with at the moment, sir,' Shaffenbeck continued. 'More than forty ships of the line plus twice as many escorts have mustered here, and from the general order signal we received we might expect as many again to join us over the coming weeks. Lord High Admiral Lansung seems to be bringing in almost everybody except the Fleet Solar to combat these latest ork attacks.'

'Being busy is no excuse to make exceptions to protocol and chain of command,' argued Kulik, though with little conviction. He dropped his voice so that only the first lieutenant could hear. 'I do not answer to Lansung's little lapdog, Admiral Acharya. He can shout at the coreward flotilla all he likes. We're from rimward command and I take direct orders only from Admiral Price.'

'Price is not favoured by the Lord High Admiral since his outburst at Caollon, sir.' The lieutenant instinctively matched his commander's informality with lowered voice. 'If the rumours are true that Price intends to make the *Colossus* his flagship when he arrives, we would do well not to rile Acharya unduly beforehand. Forgive any forwardness on my part, but I've been caught between a feuding captain and flag-captain before and it was unpleasant. I've no desire to go one step further and be batted between warring admirals.' He paused for a moment and glanced at the navigational display. 'On top of that, I certainly would prefer it if you didn't crash *Colossus* into anything.'

Kulik grunted a grudging affirmative.

'Very good, sir,' Lieutenant Shaffenbeck said, raising his voice. 'Helm, lay in course to berth sigma-seven. Comms, relay the captain's acceptance of orbital command's new instructions. Also, please conduct the captain's gratitude to the commander of *Endeavour* and extend invitation for him to join us at officers' mess at his earliest convenience.'

Kulik coughed and raised his hand to his mouth to conceal a smile at this last impertinence. Shaffenbeck was like a mother sometimes, always keen for his captain to smooth ruffled feathers and make new friends.

Even so, after a four-year wilderness on space patrol some fresh conversation at the captain's table would be very much welcomed.

TWO

Terra – the Imperial Palace

There were few settings more fitting for a war council than the Hall of Glories. A dome nearly five hundred feet across and three hundred high, buttressed and cross-vaulted like a castle tower, the Hall of Glories was the site, so it was claimed, of Rogal Dorn's meetings with his fellow primarchs on the eve of the Siege of the Imperial Palace.

It struck Drakan Vangorich, Grand Master of Assassins, that a chamber known as the Hall of Glories might be filled with all kinds of tacky trophies and paraphernalia of past victories, but it was not. It was currently only dimly lit by a few bluish glow-strips, set in alcoves flanking each of three immense double doors. The walls were granite decorated with horizontal bands of Sivalik sandstone that had been carved with frescoes of warriors stretching back through the long annals of history and prehistory.

The first time Vangorich had come to the Hall of Glories he had marvelled at the sheer inventiveness of mankind's ability to kill. The earliest figures had simple stakes hardened in fires, through various flint weapons, to the first matchlock guns and then warriors with faceted armour sporting the precursors to the lasguns of the Imperial Army. The last figures in the evolution of mankind's warriors were tall, stave-bearing soldiers not unlike the Lucifer Blacks that had become famous during the Heresy War.

Vangorich had always wondered why the fresco did not contain images of the Adeptus Astartes, nor the Custodians that guarded the Emperor. Perhaps genetically engineered transhumans had not been part of the artist's instruction, or perhaps their artificial nature rendered them disqualified from an expression of *humanity's* martial history.

There were no banners or plaques to obscure the walls in celebration of past wars. Instead, the polished black and grey marble of the floor was inscribed with a spiralling line of names picked out in gilded letters: the names of places where the Emperor's servants had fought and died. Not even victories, just planets and starships, orbital stations and drifting hulks, where blood had been shed in the cause of the Imperium and its immortal ruler.

Before the current crisis the list of battles had circled the massive hall thrice, many of them dating back to the Heresy War. Since events at Ardamantua the small army of masons and gilders had been working day and night to keep up with the litany of engagements. They had been dismissed for the war council, as had most of the functionaries and hangers-on associated with the High Lords, leaving just a few dozen record keepers, secretariats and minor members of the Senatorum Imperialis.

It irked Vangorich that he was amongst those that were

now waiting in the hall, alongside a few of the less favoured High Lords. It irked him even as it favoured him in some ways. The lesser peons of Terra were the perfect cover for an Assassin. Vangorich was unremarkable in build or appearance, save for the duelling scar that slashed through the left side of his lips and chin, and curiously wide-set, dark eyes. His simple black attire – from short boots, stockings and breeches to coat and thin scarf – was not out of place amongst the drab robes and similar suits of the flunkies and scriptors that milled about waiting for the true High Lords to arrive.

Lansung's manoeuvring had grown bolder and bolder over the last few weeks as, one by one, the other institutions that made up the Imperium – or were allied to it, in the case of the Adeptus Mechanicus – realised just how dependant they were on the benevolence of the Imperial Navy. The arrival of the Beast and the tide of battle driven before the xenos war leader had swallowed up whole star systems, and the reach of the orks seemed almost limitless. Dozens of worlds had fallen to the haphazard onslaught, and only the Navy could provide the means to stem the encroaching horde; only the Navy offered protection for important dignitaries with the means to flee before the green mass.

The Lord High Admiral had not been idle in despatching his forces to the aid of those loyal to him in the Senatorum, while those reluctant few whose support had been tardy found their outposts and convoys bereft of military support. Though the Adeptus Mechanicus had their own ships, and were essential to the maintenance of Lansung's continued dominance, it appeared the Lord High Admiral and the Fabricator General had come to an arrangement of sorts. The Lord of Mars was happy for the Master of the Fleet to take the glory, while in secret they divided the spoils of their newly-founded partnership.

A distant sounding of a fanfare heralded the coming of the major players in the Senatorum Imperialis. A column of Lucifer Blacks two abreast, the bodyguard of the Imperial elite, advanced along the corridor approaching the Hall of Glories, the crash of their tread resounding in unison. Vangorich stopped himself from showing the contempt he felt at that moment. The original Lucifer Blacks had fought during the Unification and Heresy War and earned great distinction for their loyalty and expertise. The Imperial Guardsmen in the regiment that now bore their name were little more than highly-trained, well-equipped ornaments for the grandiose. While nominally they answered to Lord Commander Militant Verreault – an upright, credible veteran whom Vangorich actually admired – the truth was that Solar-General Sayitora hired them out like mercenaries in exchange for favour and physical reward.

Each Lucifer Black wore enamelled black carapace armour over a deep woven mesh of anti-ballistic threads. Those that entered the hall bore shock-glaives – long polearms with silvered blades. Tall helms and mirrored visors concealed their faces. Their presence, in such numbers, demonstrated not only Lansung's personal resources but also signified unity between the Imperial Navy and the Astra Militarum.

This was a dangerous thing to Vangorich and he was surprised the other High Lords had allowed it to come to pass, jeopardising their own positions. Such displays of cooperation would have been unthinkable a century ago. The Imperial Army had been disbanded, the Legiones Astartes broken asunder, to prevent any one individual wielding the overwhelming power of fleet and ground troops. Now Lansung was flouting such measures, using the ork attacks as an excuse to override the old arguments and objections to such hoarding of military force.

Four hundred strong, the Lucifer Blacks split to move around the circumference of the large chamber, a score remaining by the open doors with blades raised to form an honour arch for the entering senators.

Lansung was the last to arrive, a roll and crash of drums and the climax of the clarions announcing his presence. Above, amongst the smog of incense that hung constantly beneath the dome, vast chandeliers carved as flights of ribbon-trailing cherub-like figures holding burning torches blazed into light, banishing the gloom that had previously filled the room.

Into this brightness stepped Lansung, the medals on his broad chest glinting, the gold of his brocade glistening.

Though still corpulent, the Lord High Admiral's considerable frame showed signs of being slowly eroded by his busy schedule of late. His jowls hung a little looser, his chins wobbled a little more with skin than fat. Vangorich estimated that Lansung had lost twenty, perhaps as much as twenty-five pounds, in recent weeks, and wondered whether the stress of such politicking was taking a toll in other ways. Whatever the cause, the loss of weight could not be overlooked. Certain compounds, toxins, stimulants and soporifics had to be administered in precise doses relating to the target's body mass and Vangorich would have to take this into account if his plan for the coming conference did not bear fruit and more drastic measures became necessary.

It was no coincidence that Lord High Admiral Lansung had chosen this venue for his announcement. Probably more than half of the names circling the hall were of starships; such was the nature of war in an interstellar empire. The echo back to Dorn holding council with his brothers was also a striking image to be exploited.

With a magnanimous wave of a ringed hand Lansung invited his fellow High Lords to sit down at the ornate table sitting somewhat lost in the middle of the vast chamber. Vangorich found his place towards one end amongst the other lesser participants, though this was of no surprise. He had always been fascinated by the physical representations of more abstract concepts like power and influence, and the seating arrangements of any Senatorum conclave were a study in the principles.

Somewhat more surprisingly, Lansung chose not to sit at the head of the table as Vangorich had expected, but settled between Tobris Ekharth, the Master of the Administratum, and the Speaker for the Chartist Captains, Juskina Tull. They were close enough to the head of the table to make it clear they were in ascendance, but nobody claimed the empty chair that would once have been occupied by the Sigillite or Dorn during their long councils.

On reflection, Lansung's positioning made some sense. Vangorich knew that the head of the Imperial Navy was about to announce a fresh offensive against the tide of orks encroaching upon the Segmentum Solar – and assumed the other High Lords were equally informed – and such an expedition would require considerable supplies and logistical support. By choosing to associate himself with the Administratum that would provide those supplies and the merchant fleet that would carry them, Lansung was elevating the status of both organisations above even the Astra Militarum and the Adeptus Arbites who had thus far been waging much of the fight against the barbarous greenskins.

Sat on the opposite side, at the far end, Vangorich's own position was almost as far away from Lansung as was possible whilst still remaining at the table. Only poor Hektor Rosarind, the Chancellor for Imperial Estates, was further away from the seat of power.

The chair to the right of the Assassin was empty; the Inquisitorial Representative, Wienand, was not present. Her absence annoyed Vangorich more than the admiral's posturing. He had figured she would be an easy ally to win during the coming council. Of almost equal measure was his annoyance that Wienand's chief aide and bodyguard, Raznick, had managed to disappear. He had a suspicion, but no evidence as yet, that Raznick had been sent to Mars; no doubt to make inquiries regarding Vangorich's ongoing operations at the heart of the Cult Mechanicus.

The Grand Master had at least hoped to see Wienand's public assistant on Terra, Rendenstein. She was proving as elusive as her mistress. The Inquisitorial Representative was being far more cautious since Beast Krule had killed her last second.

Lansung made no pretence of allowing the Lord Commander or the Head of the Administratum to open the proceedings. This was his war council and he rose up, hands balled into fists on the age-worn wood, and looked up and down the length of the table. There was a chorus of mechanical whines as vox-trackers were powered to catch the coming oration, while flashes from pictograph-capture units reflected from the marble columns and dark walls as the scene was recorded for posterity by the Senatorum's recollection scribes.

'In each age of man there comes a time when we are most sorely tested,' Lansung began, speaking quietly, with forced gravitas and sincerity. 'I beg leave to bring forth a motion before the Senatorum Imperialis that will define this age, and humbly lay upon the deliberations of those gathered here such meagre thoughts as I can collect on the subject that vexes us most at this time.'

Vangorich wanted to laugh – there was nothing humble or meagre about Lansung – but he kept perfectly silent and still, seemingly fixed upon the Lord High Admiral while in fact he gauged the reactions and temperament of the other High Lords.

'The encroachment of the orks staggered us, I admit. These savages we thought broken, scattered and of little conse-quence. Like many others, I allowed hopes of peace to outweigh distrust and conscience of duty. Their remark-able offensive has caught us off-guard. Even the might of the Imperial Fists, the honoured defenders of Terra itself, has been insufficient to match this threat.'

A few of the senators drew in sharp breaths. Vangorich was amazed that Lansung would openly criticise one of the First Founding Chapters as he seemed to be doing.

'We must not allow ourselves to be intimidated by the presence of these armoured ork stations in unexpected places behind our lines. If they are behind our forces, we are also at many points fighting actively behind theirs. Both sides are therefore in an extremely dangerous position. And if the Imperial Guard and our own Navy are well handled, as I believe they will be – if the brave Navy retain that genius for recovery and counter-attack for which they have so long been famous, and if the Imperial Guard shows the dogged endurance and solid fighting power of which there have been so many examples in the past – then a sudden transformation of the scene might spring into being.'

This intrigued Vangorich even further. There had been consistent whispers that Lansung was organising a fresh offensive using the fleet he was gathering at Lepidus Prime, but was he really going to openly promise a reverse of the war's fortunes?

The Lord High Admiral continued talking but Vangorich only half-listened while he considered this development. It occurred to the Grand Master of the Officio Assassinorum that Lansung was beginning to reap the rewards of promises made, but at the same time his political creditors would start demanding results. Lansung could only manipulate the situation to his advantage for so long until someone would want their payback. It was too early for any of the other senators, Vangorich especially, to accuse Lansung of overstepping the mark. However, unless the admiral could demonstrate positive movement in the situation against the orks, his backers and followers would start to fade away.

The speech he was making now signalled a transformation from a position of offering promises to actual action. Vangorich did not know what part the others were fated to play in the drama to come, or what quid pro quo had been offered to secure their support, but he could guess. The first military action would be a success for the Imperial Navy, and with that honour secured then Lansung would most likely allow the focus to shift to the Astra Militarum. Once they had gained a few victories for their rolls of honour their positions as defenders of the Imperium would be fixed for a millennium or more. History would not forget the commanders that saved the Imperium from the predations of the Beast.

'In the meantime, we shall not waste our breath nor cumber our thought with reproaches.' Lansung intertwined his pudgy fingers and nodded sagely for the benefit of the recorders. 'When you have a friend and comrade at whose side you have faced tremendous struggles, and your friend is smitten down by a stunning blow, it may be necessary to make sure that the weapon that has fallen from his hands shall not be added to the resources of your common enemy. But you need not bear malice because of your friend's cries of delirium and gestures of agony. You must not add to his pain – you must work for his recovery. The association of interest between the Imperium and the Adeptus Mechanicus remains. The cause remains. Duty inescapable remains. Subject to the iron demands of the war that we are now waging against the Beast and all his works, we shall try so to conduct ourselves towards the liberation of those benighted systems from the foulest thralldom into which they have been cast.'

Lansung paused and sipped from a crystal goblet. Water, not wine, Vangorich noted. The Lord High Admiral had seemingly sagged under the weight of responsibility during the last part of his speech, burdened by regret of mistakes past. Now he straightened and even smiled.

'Let us think rather of the future. Today is the sixth of Septival, the anniversary of the liberation of Nastor Primus. A year ago at Nastor I watched the stately parade down the Avenue of Concord by the Nastoran regiments while craft of the Navy from their shipyards flew overhead. Who can foresee what the course of the rest of the year will bring?'

The Lord High Admiral looked at Ecclesiarch Mesring, head of the freshly recognised Adeptus Ministorum. The two men exchanged friendly smiles, pre-arranged it was clear to see, intended to send another message to the doubters. Lansung had the backing of the holiest of the Emperor's servants. In return, Vangorich guessed, the Ecclesiarchy's missionaries and preachers would find welcome and passage on the ships of the Imperial Navy. It seemed that Mesring was willing to call bluff on the poison Vangorich had introduced to his system. It was also entirely possible that the Ecclesiarch had discovered a counter-agent. For the moment it did not matter – Mesring was confident enough in his continued survival to make open alliance with Lansung.

'Faith is given to us to help and comfort us when we stand in awe before the unfurling scroll of human destiny,' continued Lansung. 'And I proclaim my faith that some of us will live to see a sixth of Septival when a liberated Nastor Primus will once again rejoice in her greatness and in her glory, and once again stand forward as the champion of the freedom and the rights of man. When the day dawns, as dawn it will, the soul of all mankind will turn with comprehension and with kindness to those men and women, wherever they may be, who in the darkest hour did not despair of the Imperium.

'But let us not speak of darker days: let us speak rather of sterner days. These are not dark days, these are great days – the greatest days our people have ever lived – and we must all thank the Emperor that we have been allowed, each of us according to our stations, to play a part in making these days memorable in the history of our race.'

The admiral waited for the applause such a speech deserved, which was started by Juskina Tull and quickly taken up by the others, including Vangorich. When the clapping started to falter, Lansung sat down, stern-faced, and held up a hand in false modesty.

'Much gratitude, much gratitude. It is you that I should applaud, for allowing me to voice the thoughts of this council.'

Vangorich quickly reviewed the speech and came to the conclusion that although Lansung had spoken for some time, he had said very little at all, except as coded promises or concessions to those waiting to hear particular phrases. There had to be more here than the Master of Assassins understood, for Lansung could not advance the Navy's plans with more rhetoric; something of substance had to be forthcoming.

Vangorich decided to move the agenda along a little.

'Wonderful, Lord High Admiral! Bravo!' Lansung had been

turning towards Ekharth of the Administratum, expecting the first reply from him, but Vangorich interrupted, eliciting a brief scowl from the Navy commander.

'Thank you,' said Lansung with a gracious nod of acceptance. He started to turn back to Ekharth, who was opening his mouth to speak, but Vangorich was again quicker.

'I can barely wait for your triumphant return, Admiral Lansung.'

'Return?' Lansung was perplexed more than vexed. 'What return?'

'Well, we all know that you wield starships as well as you weave words, Lord High Admiral, as befits your station. I assumed that you would be personally leading the fleet against the ork menace.'

Eyes narrowed for a moment, Lansung saw the trap being laid out for him. With an agility of thought far beyond any physical act he might perform, the admiral side-stepped quickly.

'To conceive of the plan that will bring us victory will be reward enough, Master Vangorich. Like yourself, I would rather not draw attention to my efforts. There are many fine admirals in the Segmentum Solar deserving of a chance to earn proper respect and renown without my interference.'

Vangorich knew that his first strike had been hasty and clumsy and he regretted the attempt even as he smiled at the Lord High Admiral. His mind was racing, seeking some parry to Lansung's counter-argument.

'Noble, very noble, admiral. Yet your modesty endangers the Imperium. I would not have us send a lesser commander simply for the sake of history's recognition. One does not leave a better balanced and sharper blade in its sheath because others have not seen such frequent use, and I think you do yourself a disservice by squandering your capacities here in the Senatorum when battle calls to your most precious talents.'

Lansung's fixed smile grew genuine and Vangorich realised that he had missed his mark again. The admiral clearly knew that if he was physically removed from Terra his grip on the Senatorum would be lessened. Vangorich was trying to prise just a little finger away from the vice-like fist that Lansung currently maintained, and the benefit of inter-stellar distance would be considerable. There was even the chance that he might actually die in battle, though every-thing Vangorich knew about Lansung suggested he was vain and ambitious, but never a physical coward. His ser-vice record was very impressive, as was the ruthlessness that underpinned it, and Vangorich would not be able to make any accusation of that ilk. The admiral knew this and easily deflected the suggestion.

'The commanders that will be chosen will have served under me for many years, Grand Master.'

I bet they have, thought Vangorich.

'It is they who have been serving directly against the foes of mankind these past years and are best placed to enact our strategies against the Beast,' Lansung continued. 'A degree of detachment, physical as well as emotional, is required for command, my dear Vangorich. I would have thought you understood that as well as those of us who have war in our blood.'

Vangorich had to concede the point with a superficial nod.

He was irked again that Wienand was not there to exploit what he could not see, but there was no point wasting time wishing for things that were not to be. The eyes of the other High Lords were upon him, showing a mixture of sympathy and impatience. He would not be indulged much longer and had to take a different approach.

'I must defer to your superior wisdom in this instance, admiral.' Vangorich took a petty but encouraging satisfaction from the tic of annoyance in Lansung's eye whenever the Grand Master did not use his full title. No matter what happened next, Vangorich could still get inside Lansung's head when he needed to. 'Like the others, I am on tenterhooks. Please, furnish us with the details of your plans so that we might debate and approve them.'

'When the latest intelligence has been compiled, I shall lay before this council every facet of the coming strategy.' This was pure dissembling and Vangorich knew that he had lost this round. 'Until such a time, I would think it wise that the council airs its desires and aims for the coming offensive, so that the voice of all shall be heard and taken into account.'

This was nothing short of open invitation for the assembled senators to bring out every time-worn axe to grind again, to air every slight and disagreement brought forth in previous gatherings.

Vangorich stifled a sigh of boredom. This was going to be a long council. He would be sure to make Wienand regret her decision to be absent.

THREE

Immaterium – Subservius

Aboard the Adeptus Mechanicus ship there was stalemate.

'Out of the question, Captain Koorland,' said Magos Biologis Eldon Urquidex. The tech-priest's telescopic eyes lengthened an inch, the closest equivalent to a glare that the man could muster. Secondary tool appendages waved disapprovingly around his midriff. 'In the absence of data the most obvious course of action is your transit to Terra, or perhaps Mars. You are, in no vacillating terms, the last of your Chapter. Not only is your physical personage highly valued, both for physiological investigation and purposes of wider military morale, but your first-hand experiences of this latest orkoid threat are invaluable. There is, to be clear, nobody else like you in the galaxy at this moment in time. To even consider returning you to a position of active combat duty would be reprehensible.'

Koorland towered over the tech-priest, even without his armour, and was quite capable of ripping apart his heavily augmented and cybertised adversary, but Urquidex stared up at the gigantic warrior without any sign of fear. Small digital tools flickered in and out of the tech-priest's fingertips as Urquidex interlaced his hands across his barrel chest.

Captain Koorland turned back towards the viewport. Outside was a field of stars, the very edge of the system. In a day or two they would reach the Mandeville point and be clear for translation into warp space. The Space Marine's reflection was dark-skinned, almost blackened by the melanchromic reflex that had protected him from the radiation that had killed so many of his battle-brothers.

'You must understand that I will not allow that to happen, magos,' Koorland said heavily. He laid a hand against the wall, fingers splayed, as if reaching out to the dead they were leaving behind. 'I am a Space Marine. It is my duty to fight.'

'It is your duty to serve the Emperor, second captain, and you can best do your duty by returning to the Sol System with us to divulge all intelligence you have gathered on the nature of this menace. In the longer term that will be of far greater benefit to the Imperium you are sworn to protect.'

'Logically, perhaps.' Koorland swung around to confront the tech-priest. 'I would not expect you to understand the creed of the warrior-born, the oath of the Wall.'

'If such matters are illogical, as you say, then your assumption is correct, second captain.' Urquidex slumped slightly, his mechanical appendages drooping a little. A look approximating pity crossed what remained of his face, as though some more primitive, biological part of the man-machine was now in control. 'Do not think me totally impervious to your predicament. Thousands of the Machine-God's servants have perished here, and millions more across many star systems. They gave their lives to improve our chances of victory at some future point. Unless we are to throw untold billions of lives at this problem and hope to defeat the orks' raw aggression with untamed barbarity of our own, we must learn to fight more intelligently. At the moment we are outmatched on both accounts.'

'What do you mean by that?' Koorland crossed the small cell-like chamber and sat on the fold-down cot along one wall. It sagged under his weight, the reinforced braces creaking. 'Let me tell you, my brothers and I fought with courage, honour and discipline. There was nothing we could do to match the power of the attack moon.'

'My point exactly, captain.' Urquidex paused as the door hissed open.

Standing on the threshold was a mostly mechanical apparition, which Koorland at first took to be a servitor.

'Good evening, Captain Koorland,' said the thing, in a voice that had the thrum of artificial modulation but was unmistakably that of Phaeton Laurentis.

'Emperor's Throne!' swore Koorland, standing up. 'What happened to you?'

The tech-priest looked nothing like he had the first time Koorland had met him. He now stepped through the doorway on a tripod of legs, his mechanical lower torso clanking and whirring with pistons in an effort to maintain balance. Most of Laurentis' upper body was covered with his robes but beneath their thick layer were unnatural bulges and twists of hidden cables, jutting pipes and trembling implants. His arms were double-articulated miniature cranes, tipped with quad-digit grabbing claws that clacked open and shut as Laurentis raised a hand in greeting. Nothing remained of his face except for a small patch of flesh and one eye, which had been relocated to a central position. The rest was heavily riveted metal plates, speaker grilles and sensor-cluster lenses and spines.

'My physique has undergone a number of repairs and upgrades. No cause for alarm.'

'When I saw most of you splayed out on that examination gurney I thought they would put you back together the way you had been.'

'There were some very inefficient systems in that body,' said Urquidex before Laurentis could offer an opinion either way. 'Magos Laurentis' newly adapted form is far better for the sort of tasks he will be performing.'

'That sounds like a demotion,' said Koorland, sitting down again now that his surprise had subsided. 'Have you offended your superiors in some way, tech-priest?'

'The offence is to the Machine-God,' said Laurentis. 'I perhaps spoke out of turn concerning the actions of my fellow techna-liturgia during the Ardamantua crisis. Only by thorough debriefing have I been allowed to continue in the role of magos. However, this body and these duties of which my colleague speaks are not a punishment. Most of my flesh was destroyed and many of my hard-lined systems corrupted. Fortunately my core data store remained intact.'

'If I understand it right, I have you to thank, what little it is worth, for my life.'

'Gratitude is not required, captain. I simply acted on a most illogical stimulus.' The construct-man's head rotated strangely to regard Urquidex with a cluster of red lenses. 'I believe I have formulated a new axiom of research.'

'Indeed?' exclaimed the magos biologis. 'That would be unprecedented. Are you quite sure that your faculties remained intact following your violent interaction with the orkoids?'

'It is called a "battle", magos. Not a "violent interaction". I know; I was involved in it.' Koorland could not help but feel some amusement at the irony of this statement. It was Laurentis that had once called the Chromes' claws 'digital blades affixed to or articulated from forelimbs'. Though his body had been rendered even more artificial and mechanical, Laurentis' personality seemed to have lurched towards the biological.

'This axiom, I am very proud of it,' Laurentis continued. 'Perhaps if it is adopted it shall be named after me. And this is it: "When all rational explanation has been exhausted, any explanation, no matter how irrational, must be the solution." Do you like it?'

'Nonsensical drivel of the highest order. It was exactly this unbecoming manner that brought censure from Magos Van Auken.'

'By all rational explanation, there were no survivors of Ardamantua. Yet here you are, captain.' Laurentis returned his attention to the Space Marine. 'My own recollection, somewhat hazily rendered by my damaged editicore processors, is of acting not out of any extant proof that you were alive, or indeed that there were any other survivors. Not as far as I was consciously aware. In my fragmentary state I believe I happened upon a further stage of enlightenment concerning the artifices of the Machine-God. Through unconscious and subconscious deduction I formed the illogical hypothesis that someone might be alive. My adjustment of the scanning parameters was equally unfounded by rational deduction.'

'A guess,' said Urquidex. 'Random extrapolation of chaos. The Machine-God works in a convoluted manner, Laurentis, but if you believe that you are some new prophet of his artifice I must disappoint you. Evidently you have suffered a deeper malfunction to your core centres than we believed.'

'A hunch,' said Koorland. He shook his head in disbelief. 'A tech-priest acted on an instinct, a hunch? It seems Ardamantua was remarkable in one more respect.'

'Quite so,' said Laurentis. Two of his sensor antennae bent upwards in something that might have been an attempt at a smile. 'A hunch.'

'It would be in your interest not to announce such a thing in the presence of Van Auken,' said Urquidex. 'He is already minded to have you core-stripped and data-mined for all information regarding the events at Ardamantua. This heretical nonsense does no credit to your continued deterministic existence, Laurentis.'

'That will not happen,' said Koorland. 'Though Magos Laurentis does not acknowledge his efforts, I do, and I am bound by my traditions to honour the debt I owe to him. There will be no punitive measures or investigations carried out, do you understand?'

'It is not your place to interfere in an internal matter of the Adeptus Mechanicus, captain. Your opinion in this matter is inconsequential.' Despite his words there was a note of equivocation in the tech-priest's tone.

Koorland stood up, his head nearly brushing the ceiling of the recuperation cell. Without seeming to expend any effort at all, the Space Marine grabbed Urquidex's robes in a massive fist and lifted the magos from the deck. Koorland turned so that Urquidex was pressed up against the yards-thick glass of the viewport. The magos' mechadendrites and bionic limbs squirmed.

'Perhaps you will find floating in vacuum of no consequence, magos,' said the captain. 'That will be your fate should I learn of anything befalling Magos Laurentis. Equal unpleasantness will ensue for Van Auken or anyone else that acts against the interest of the magos. Am I understood?'

Urquidex nodded. Koorland lowered the tech-priest and relinquished his grasp.

'Very well. You may leave now.'

Without another word Urquidex scuttled out of the room, head and appendages bobbing with disapproval. Koorland watched the tech-priest disappear down the corridor outside and then sat down once the magos had turned out of view. He realised that Laurentis was regarding him with a full suite of sensors, his one remaining eye staring directly at the Space Marine.

'Interesting,' said the tech-priest.

'What is?'

'Though not intimately acquainted with every battle-custom and facet of Chapter orthodoxy concerning the Imperial Fists, my data-files were significantly invested with relevant material before my association with your warriors began. I do not recall any specific blood-debt traditions or requirements, the likes of which you appear to have invoked. That being the case, in absence of other evidence, I assume that you have taken it upon yourself to extend a protective oath in my favour for another reason. I am at a loss to explain what that reason might be.'

Koorland leaned forwards, thick forearms resting on his knees.

'Let us just call it a hunch.'

FOUR

Terra – the Imperial Palace

The Sigillite's Retreat.

Vangorich wondered if the small walled garden had been named as a place of repose for the founder of the Council of Terra, or if it perhaps drew on an even more ancient history for its inspiration.

The area was square, about thirty foot across, quite unimposing by the standards of the Imperial Palace. A single log split in two down its length and shaped by carpenters formed a cross-shaped bench at the centre of the garden, at a diagonal to the four archways by which the cloister could be entered. The paths were of pure white gravel between beds of larger stones in dark grey and black, arranged something like a floor plan, though Vangorich suspected a purpose more symbolic or metaphysical informed the layout.

The Grand Master wondered if there had once been plants here. If so, they had died long ago for lack of care; no mouldering leaf or root, or speck of soil remained amongst the sterile rock.

Like many other parts of the Palace, the Sigillite's Retreat had been cut off by collapsed bastions and fallen walls, isolated by the ruin brought down upon Terra during the Heresy War. Only a chance remark in one of the old annals even admitted its existence, and it had taken three whole years of diligent investigation for Vangorich to identify its position, and a further six to secretly excavate and conceal passage into the garden.

Overhead must once have been open to the sky, but now the only light was dim, filtered through a dirty window mesh dome in the roof of the greater Palace nearly half a mile above. If one looked above the twenty-foot-high walls, the towering edifice of the Palace crowded down, piled up on great columns floor after floor, a teetering mass of dormitories and offices for the Administratum. It was if the garden existed in its own little bubble of reality now, a cave amongst the strata of hab-complexes and scriptoria.

But here in the midst of the bureaucracy and madness was a place of utter charm and utter calm. It was all the more precious to Vangorich because only he knew of its existence. The volume that named the space had been hidden deep within the Librarius Sanctus where nobody else would find it; the convicted criminal labourers sequestered from the Adeptus Arbites had been handed over to the Adeptus Mechanicus for induction as servitors after they had completed their work.

Alone, quiet and undisturbed, Vangorich sat on the wooden bench and considered his options without risk of discovery. It was perhaps the only place in the galaxy he lessened his guard for a moment.

It was, therefore, something of a shock to the Grand Master to hear a delicate cough behind him.

He was on his feet in a moment, las-blade flicked from his sleeve, digital weapons glinting with power as he flexed his knuckles in preparation to fire.

Wienand stood leaning against the inside of one of the arches, her arms crossed, her face a mask of smugness. Her features were young for one of her position, though anti-agapics and age-reducing therapies were a possibility. She was not quite as tall as Vangorich, of athletic build, with short, pale grey hair and a narrow, sharp-boned face. Not unpleasant to look at by any measure, but also not so pretty that she would attract undue attention at a gathering.

She was dressed in a dirty coveralls, much patched, over a chunky shirt of grey canvas-like fabric. Workman's boots and an oily rag spilling from a pocket completed the disguise. Vangorich realised she must have been forced to masquerade as a menial in order to gain entry to his refuge. He didn't know exactly where the security breach was, but that fact alone narrowed it down to a few possibilities.

'Surprise,' said the Inquisitorial Representative, showing pearl-white teeth in a grin.

'Surprise be damned, you wretched woman,' snapped Vangorich, rattled for the first time in many decades. 'I might have killed you.'

'Now, now, Grand Master, at least have the grace to admit when you have been outdone.'

Vangorich sheathed his blade and deactivated the

digi-weapons. He conceded the point with a single nod of the head and gestured Wienand towards the bench.

'It was too much to hope that I might be permitted just a single place of sanctuary,' he said, sitting down while Wienand advanced along the path, the gravel scrunching under her tread. The noise brought fresh irritation; a reminder of the peace he sought being broken. Also, it was just clumsy to be heard so easily and it irked all of Vangorich's instincts for stealth.

'You can be assured that I will not tell anybody else,' she said, sitting on the bench to Vangorich's left, across from him. 'I am rather glad you have a little bolthole, Drakan. It makes me feel safer knowing that a man who puts himself under so much stress has somewhere he can relax. The last thing we need at the moment is a Grand Master of Assassins getting tetchy.'

'What do you mean by that?'

'Your little outburst during Lansung's war council. It was stupid.'

Vangorich blinked, shocked twice in a short space of time, this time by the inquisitor's bluntness. 'At least I was in attendance, in a position to oppose this disastrous plan.'

'Disastrous? Do you think there should be no response against the ork attacks? You might well think that Lansung and his games are the greatest threat to the Imperium but it is not your position to judge! The orks will not wait for us to reorganise ourselves and any response, no matter how late and no matter what the motivation behind it, must be welcome. There is an actual war, Drakan, and we are very close to losing it. Perhaps you think your operatives will be able to assassinate every one of the greenskins?'

'If Lansung gets his way, it will lead to a reunification, in practice if not law, of the Navy and Guard. Surely you can see what a threat that poses.'

'Greater than the orks? Not yet. Let us not get ahead of ourselves. We will burn that bridge when we get to it. You really are starting to overstep your mark, Drakan. While you were busy destroying whatever credibility you had left by responding to Lansung's posturing, I have been hard at work protecting the Imperium. Your meddling is causing more problems than it is solving. In fact, have you done anything useful lately? I know you have a cell on Mars, do they have anything to report?'

In no mood for banter, Vangorich stood up, straightened his coat and started walking towards the archway ahead.

'If you leave, you will never find out what I was going to tell you,' said the inquisitor.

Vangorich stopped at the arch but did not turn. 'Really? Do you think me such a useful hound that you can feed me scraps at your whim to keep me loyal?'

'I bring a warning.'

Turning, Vangorich raised an eyebrow in inquiry.

'Yes, a warning,' said Wienand, standing up. 'You are making enemies, Drakan. Powerful enemies.'

'That is not news, my dear Wienand.' Vangorich smiled with genuine amusement. 'How nice of you to care for my well-being.'

'It is the Inquisition that you are starting to alienate, Grand Master.'

Vangorich kept his tone light, hiding the concern he felt at this statement.

'I thought we were friends, Wienand. I know we have had our odd duel, but we are allies, are we not?'

'And that is your other mistake. We are allies for the time being, of a sort, but do not think for a moment that I place any concern for you above the greater protection of the Emperor and the Imperium. We would use and discard each other in an instant, do not pretend otherwise.'

'My other mistake?'

'Your first is to conflate the Inquisitorial Representative with the Inquisition. I am not a Lord High Admiral, a Grand Master, not even a speaker. My position is entirely arbitrary, sustained by the goodwill of my fellow inquisitors and no small amount of political games I must play away from the Senatorum. There are many who are beginning to doubt the wisdom of my continued presence in that role.'

'It sounds as if you have enemies, not I. I wish you every fortune in your future endeavours away from the Senatorum Imperialis.'

'You vain idiot, shut up and listen!'

The words were like a slap across the face, sharp and stinging. Vangorich took a step towards Wienand, hand half-raised to strike her. He gathered his temper and turned the fist into a pointing finger.

'Pick your words carefully, inquisitor, if you wish to retain such allies as you currently possess. It seems to me that you come seeking help but cloak it as threat.'

'There is movement against me within the Inquisition on two fronts, Drakan. Firstly, they believe I have been too tolerant of the excesses of the Senatorum during recent events. In fact they feel that the entire Imperium's governance has been allowed to fall to ruin in the past few decades. They want to extend a stronger, more obvious control over the Senatorum.'

'The Inquisition may have absolute authority, but they cannot survive without the cooperation of the likes of Lansung, Zeck and Gibran. Your temporal power is limited by the resources others place at your disposal.'

'There are some that forget such truth. They believe, in no small part due to the influence of the Ministorum, that they answer a genuine calling by the Emperor. Righteous men and women make for dangerous rulers.'

'There is another reason for your position becoming more precarious?'

'My treatment of you, Grand Master. The Officio Assassinorum is a weapon to be deployed at the behest of the High Lords, not an organisation to sit in judgement of them. Some amongst my order wish to make an example of you and your temples.'

'We would retaliate.'

'If you wish to plunge the Imperium into anarchy whilst it is beset from outside by xenos of untold destructive potential. They rely upon you, Drakan, to stay true to your loyalty and duty.'

Vangorich was about to reply, but held his tongue. Could he really fall on his own sword to protect the greater stability of the Imperium? Was he that dedicated? More importantly, did these mysterious inquisitors believe that he would, and so risk everything on the presumption?

'I see that you begin to understand the gravity of our situation.' Wienand watched him intently as she stepped closer, dropping her voice. 'We must indulge in a brief period of mutual preservation. That is why I have come here, to your inner sanctuary. I declare amnesty. You will have my full cooperation if you promise me yours.'

There was no way Vangorich could take her at her word, but conversely his own promise would be equally meaningless, so why did she ask for it? Was she really that scared of what the Inquisition, or at least parts of it, intended to do?

'All right, an amnesty for the moment. Better that we exert ourselves to the frustration of Lansung's ambitions than expend energy circling each other without effect. What did you have in mind?'

Wienand laid a hand on Vangorich's shoulder as she stepped even closer.

'Your aim is good, Grand Master. If we can force Lansung out into the fleet there is a chance that we can repair some of the damage he has done in the Senatorum in his absence. We might even get very lucky and he'll be blasted by the orks. However, simple argument is not going to be enough. Events, my dear Drakan, will have to conspire to force the admiral to move his fat hindquarters onto the bridge of a starship.'

'What events?'

'That is what I am here to discuss...'

FIVE

Lepidus Prime – orbital

'Remind my steward to use less starch in future,' said Kulik, fidgeting with the stiff collar of his shirt.

'I shall pass on the message,' said Shaffenbeck, in an absent-minded way that conveyed that he would do no such thing because Kulik was never happy with the starch of his collars. Throughout their time together the captain's shirts had always been understarched or overstarched depending on mood, as though there were some infinitesimally small sweet spot that he desired that no mortal could ever attain.

'And remind me never to accept an invitation to one of these gatherings,' Kulik continued. He moved his agitation to the heavy brocaded cuffs of his coat. Never comfortable in full dress uniform, the captain was sweltering, positive that rivulets of sweat were coursing down his face.

Turbine-like fans in the launch bay's ceiling spun lazily, doing little to disperse the body heat of the hundred-or-so assembled officers who had come aboard the *Defiant Monarch* at Admiral Acharya's 'request.' Kulik knew as well as every other commodore, captain and commander present that such requests were not ignored without good reason. As well as the visiting ship commanders, each with their seconds and some with other hangers-on, there were nearly two dozen lesser officers from the *Defiant Monarch* and the same number again of petty officers marshalling the small army of attendants serving drinks and food.

'Wine or water?' asked Shaffenbeck, accosting a passing steward.

'Both,' growled Kulik. A moment later a fluted glass of bubbling white wine was in his right hand. The captain swiftly downed the contents and the empty glass was exchanged for a stein of almost clear water. Surprised, Kulik sniffed the contents. It didn't smell of anything. He cocked an eye at Shaffenbeck. 'Non-reclaimed hydrates? The admiral really is trying to impress us.'

'Tenders were moving about thirty thousand litres of the stuff from Lepidus this past week,' said Shaffenbeck. Kulik knew he could rely on the lieutenant to be abreast of everything going on around the fleet. It was the main reason he overlooked his second-in-command's abuse of the command comms channel, which by regulations was for the ship's captain only.

'And what of the admiral himself?'

Saul nodded to the left. Kulik turned and saw Acharya standing in a gaggle of attentive captains and commanders, his flag-captain Brusech like a bodyguard beside him. Acharya was an unimposing man, of average height and features. His one distinguishing mark was a scar running from his right ear to his lip, a ragged line of red against almost white skin. In contrast Brusech was a giant of a man, with a black bushy beard streaked with grey, his head covered in an unruly mop of the same. Instinctively Kulik ran a hand across his scalp, checking his hair was smoothed down.

'Stories say that the scar was suffered in combat at the hands of pirates around the Perithian Nebulae,' Shaffenbeck said.

'And less favourable tales claim Acharya fell down a flight of stairs whilst drunk,' countered Kulik. Despite his dislike of Acharya's grandstanding and obvious politicking, Kulik was inclined to favour the former explanation. 'I served with Acharya briefly on board the *Lord of Hosts*, you know?'

'I did not realise. You must have only been an ensign?'

'Not quite. I was twelfth lieutenant. Acharya was second. He was competent, fair. Nothing spectacular but nothing terrible, either. I suspect he would have made flag rank eventually, even without licking the boots of the Lord High Admiral. Was very fond of quoting Eskenstein's *Navis Tacticus Superium* every few minutes. I think he must have memorised it, but never really learnt it.'

'Ah, and here comes the other godly being,' said Shaffenbeck, stepping back slightly so that Kulik could see past him.

'Hush your blasphemy,' Kulik replied automatically.

The lieutenant's retreat revealed the crowd parting for a short but handsome man, officers peeling aside like waves at the prow of a seagoing ship. The new arrival was dressed in stark black – a rarity amongst the usual dark blue that signified a period of officer service in the prestigious Sol fleet – and wore a peaked cap that cast a deep shadow over his face from the stark lighting strips overhead.

The man nodded and smiled in response to greetings from those around him, his head moving left and right constantly as if seeking out something. His search was successful as he spied Kulik and raised a hand in greeting.

'Admiral Price,' said the captain with a nod and a slight bow.

'Rafal. Good to see you,' said Kulik's immediate superior, Admiral of the Rimward Flotilla. Price tucked his cap under his arm, revealing slightly ruffled shoulder-length blond hair, and suddenly he seemed in his late thirties rather than early fifties. He grinned, wiping away another ten years with the boyish expression. Kulik could well understand the rumours that Price embodied the Naval tradition of having a girl – several girls – at every station he visited.

'I was not expecting you, sir,' said Kulik. He glanced towards Acharya, who had noticed the appearance of his rival and was making his way through the throng in their direction.

'My invitation must have been lost in the warp somehow,' Price said with a wink. 'I'm sure Solar Baron Crziel Acharya, Admiral of the Fleet, fully intended for me to attend.'

Kulik rubbed his chin thoughtfully and turned as Acharya approached.

'Dominius, I thought you would be too busy with berthing orders and requisitions mandates,' said Acharya. His voice was slightly higher pitched than most men's, though it made up in volume what it lacked in gravitas. 'After all, I thought you loved that sort of thing. If I had known you would prise yourself away from your desk and forms I would have sent a cutter for you.'

'Such consideration would have been unnecessary,

Admiral Acharya,' Price replied evenly, ignoring the insult. 'As it is, my lighter will be taking me back to *Colossus* where I shall raise my flag.'

Kulik looked sharply at Price.

'Sorry, Rafal, here are your orders,' Price continued, slipping a small envelope from the pocket of his coat. He handed it to Kulik and then returned his attention to Acharya. 'Any word for the fleet from the Lord High Admiral yet?'

Acharya shook his head slowly. There was the brief exchange of a glance between the admiral and his flag-captain. Price noticed it too.

'I see that perhaps you are finally going to show some initiative,' said Price.

'The chain of command exists for a reason,' said Acharya. 'It would be anarchy if we all started interpreting orders to our own satisfaction. That is, as you well know, the sort of thing that would get a man relegated to a life of convoy baby-sitting and patrols to half-remembered star forts on the segmentum rim.'

Price's smile faded. He was about to speak but stopped himself, instead relieving a passing steward of a small glass of some amber-coloured liquor. He sniffed the contents of the tumbler and raised his eyebrows in surprise.

'Neoscotian whisky? The real thing?' There was genuine appreciation, perhaps even awe, in Price's voice and expression. He took a sip. 'By the Emperor, it really is!'

'A century old, and more,' Acharya said smugly, taking a glass of the same from the steward, who had stopped at Kulik's elbow. He held the drink up to the light and turned it to and fro, gold refracting onto the pale flesh of his hand.

'Thirty thousand light years from home, and still as pure as the sunlight that fell on the grain that made it.'

'If only I had known.' Price paused to gulp down the remaining contents of his glass, eliciting a wince from Acharya, who must have paid a small fortune just for one bottle of the precious alcohol. Price's eyes widened a little and he gave a slight shudder of pleasure. 'If only I had known that influence could bring such rewards, I would have started kissing Admiral Lansung's arse years ago.'

Acharya's cheeks reddened and his lips trembled with anger as he glared at Price.

'Of course,' Price continued, with some bitterness, 'I was too busy baby-sitting convoys and running supplies to half-forgotten outposts, wasn't I?'

With a snarl, Admiral Acharya turned sharply and stalked away, tossing his glass carelessly aside, the expensive liquor splashing on the deck. Brusech sighed and shook his head.

'Come on, captain,' said Price, turning in the opposite direction.

Kulik stepped to follow but was stopped by Brusech's hand on his arm. The huge man glanced left then right and then leaned down to speak softly in Kulik's ear.

'A word of warning, Rafal. Admiral Acharya has sent orders to the coreward fleet to make translation. He's going to lead a relief force to Port Sanctus.'

'Sanctus? You mean the orks haven't overrun the shipyards there yet?'

'Latest reports are that the docks and orbital platforms are still holding out. If we can break the blockade, the Sanctus sector fleet will be added to our strength.'

'So why haven't I received these orders yet?'

'Price,' said Brusech, looking over Kulik's shoulder at the receding figure of the admiral. 'Acharya wants to leave behind the rimward fleet, make it look like Price was sat on his arse twiddling his thumbs while the coreward flotillas earn the glory.'

'And how am I to know that this isn't some ploy of Acharya's to get Price to break ranks and head off on his own, earning him further scorn from the Lord High Admiral? If the admiral goes against orders again, Lansung's all but promised to have him hung for mutiny.'

'Let's not play this game, Rafal,' said Brusech. He straightened up and laid an arm across Kulik's shoulders. He smiled at the other officers milling around them and kept his voice quiet. 'You and me, we've got to keep the admirals focused, right? Believe me, I have no desire to jump into Port Sanctus with half the available ships. We don't know how strong the orks really are, but I'd rather have every gun I can and see some go unfired than go into that fight without everything we've got. Trust me, Rafal, there's no good to come of this if we don't all go.'

'And I assume you've said as much to Acharya? Cheap jibes aside, it really isn't like him to show this kind of independence. Has he received word from the Lord High Admiral?'

'No orders from Terra. I'd have seen them. I tried convincing Acharya not to go this way, but he won't listen.' Brusech shrugged, setting the tassels of his epaulettes swaying like clock pendulums. 'Seems he's taking advice from some young commodore, name of Sartinus. I don't know this

Sartinus but he's got connections back on Terra and now he's got the admiral's ear too. Acharya's claiming the plan is his own, of course, but I smell Sartinus all over it. Don't ask me why some commodore fresh out of the Sol fleet is so eager to get us to attack Port Sanctus.'

'That's all well above my station, I'm sure,' said Kulik. He offered his hand to Brusech. 'Thank you for the alert.'

'Just get Price to come along,' said the other flag-captain, shaking Kulik's hand. 'I've got a bad feeling about this.'

Brusech nodded and walked away, long strides taking him after Admiral Acharya. Saul fell in beside Kulik as the captain headed off after his superior.

'What do you make of that?' he asked the lieutenant.

'Brusech seems to be on the level,' said Shaffenbeck. 'Word around the fleet is that he's the sort of captain you want in a crunch. Dependable, straightforward, honest. Come to think of it, I've no idea what Acharya sees in him.'

'Less of that, lieutenant,' Kulik replied. 'If the admirals want to use us in their game, that's fine, but let's not choose sides.'

'I think the sides have already chosen us, sir,' Saul replied stiffly. 'Admiral Price is using the *Colossus* as flagship and Acharya wants nothing to do with the rimward fleet. I would say I know whose hand is feeding me.'

'That might be true, but Price isn't blameless. Like you say, he's decided to start playing this game too.'

'So are you going to tell him what Brusech said?'

'Certainly. It's going to be no secret when Acharya's ships leave their berths, so I'd rather not have it look like I don't know what's happening. I should have realised something was amiss when I received the invitation to this... gathering.

Most of the men here are Acharya's. A final send-off, no doubt.'

Price had been waylaid by the intervention of various junior officers looking for favour, or simply to meet one of their heroes – Price's reputation as a maverick had earned him some admirers amongst a certain type of officer. He was about to step into the corridor that joined the cleared landing bay with the neighbouring flight deck when Kulik caught up with him.

'Took your time,' said the admiral, clearly in a surly mood after his encounter with Acharya. What had probably started out as a bit of light-hearted goading in Price's mind had turned personal and sour very swiftly. 'What did that enormous oaf want with you?'

'Sir,' said Kulik, with just enough admonition in his voice that the single word had become a catch-all reproach. It was a trick he had learned from Shaffenbeck.

Price looked at him sharply, mouth curling with displeasure at the captain's tone.

'Captain Brusech is a capable officer, and we are fortunate that he is around to temper Admiral Acharya's excesses.'

'I suppose you are right,' said Price, a little petulantly. 'Anyway, what were you two conspiring about?'

Kulik related the conversation almost verbatim, while they traversed the linking corridor and entered the next flight bay. Cutters, shuttles and lighters from dozens of ships were packed into lines on either side of the exit strip. Admiral Price's was close at hand, as befitted his rank.

'We'll take the *Colossus*' cutter, mine can head back to the *Indefatigable*,' announced Price, absorbing the news from Kulik. The air crew that had been fussing around the admiral's shuttle slunk back into the gloom between the bulky craft.

They walked in silence across the deck, heading for Kulik's lighter, which had been parked somewhat further away from the main deck than was polite for an officer of his rank. Just as with the ship's berth, Admiral Acharya was displaying his disdain.

'We won't go, of course,' said Price as they reached the *Colossus'* shuttle. One of the junior lieutenants, Cabriot, oversaw the deck crew moving the boarding steps into place. Kulik said nothing as they ascended to the craft, preferring not to say anything in front of the lower ranks.

'I think that would be unwise,' said Kulik when the door to the captain's cabin had been sealed, leaving the captain, admiral and lieutenant to speak without being heard. 'That's what Acharya wants you to do. If you don't go and the relief attack fails, he can blame you for not supporting his fleet.'

'But if I do go, we'll probably win and that smug bastard will take all of the credit for the action,' replied Price. 'His decision; let him live by it or die by it.'

'And the men that serve in his fleet? Is it their decision?'

'They knew the risks when they joined up,' Price said quickly. 'We don't get to choose where the enemy are, nor where we might be required to lay down our lives.'

Kulik considered this for a moment, appalled by the sentiment. Price must have read something in his expression.

'What? You look like you've just found out your favourite port doxy has the under-pox.'

'Forgive any forwardness, but this isn't like you, admiral. That's the sort of thing I'd expect to hear from the likes of Acharya. You never struck me as a commander who sees his men as expendable. This rivalry with Acharya, it's changing you into something I don't think you intend. If we let Acharya charge off with just his fleet more men will die. Most of those ships will not come back, and you know that's true.'

Price said nothing for a little while, but sat staring at the decking. When he did speak, he was quiet, showing the humility that had earned Kulik's respect ten years earlier when they had first met.

'Sorry, Rafal.' He looked the captain in the eye and moved his gaze to Shaffenbeck. 'Your captain can be quite the moraliser, can't he? He has a keen insight at times.'

'He got that from me, admiral,' said the lieutenant, without any hint of irony or humour.

'Some of our ships are still resupplying, and the *Conqueror* and *Heavenly Wrath* are docked for refitting,' said Kulik. 'It'll take at least five days to get the rimward flotilla ready, never mind some other parts of the fleet. If Acharya intends to take his ships out for translation tomorrow, we'll be running to keep up.'

'Yes, but I can't just send my ships out piecemeal.' Price folded his arms and leaned back with eyes closed. 'We'll split the fleet into two waves. Ships ready at present, except the *Colossus*, will be seconded to Acharya's ship and leave straight away. We'll take the stragglers in the second wave.'

'You'll give command of the ships to Acharya? Isn't that what he wants?' said Saul.

'You know he'll use our ships as the vanguard if we let him, sending them in while holding back his,' added Kulik.

'*Temporary* command, gentlemen,' said Price, opening his eyes. 'But good point, Rafal. I'll set the transit order for two days' time. That should give Acharya's fleet enough of a head start.'

'Does it bother you that Acharya's forced us into this position?' asked Kulik. 'It occurs to me that perhaps I am being used by Brusech. It would be a bit of a climb-down if Acharya had to request you support him in the attack at Port Sanctus. Maybe he is relying on your better nature to follow him into battle, but this way he'll look like the leader rather than an equal.'

'Yes, to all of your points,' said Price. He pulled something from his coat pocket: a silver flask engraved with the seal of Neoscotia's Distillarius Superior. Price laughed and winked. 'I managed to swipe this from one of the stewards. Small recompense, but it'll do for now.'

Price took a swig and lifted the container in toast.

'Here's to the spoils of politics,' he said with a laugh.

Kulik took the proffered flask and laughed too. But only on the outside. The politics of admirals would soon get lots of men killed. He hoped it would be worth the sacrifice.

SIX

Nestrum – Mandeville point

'There can be no blame apportioned for your loss at Ardamantua.' Laurentis gripped a regicide piece in one of his
crane-claws and moved it across the board. He placed it
in its new position with a heavy click. 'To have forecast
the advances in technology and strategy employed by the
orks would have required extrapolation bordering upon
the insane.'

'Only a madman could have foreseen what happened
at Ardamantua?' replied Koorland. He studied the regicide board. Sixteen days it had taken for the ship to travel
to Nestrum, where they now waited to rendezvous with
another vessel. The *Achilles* was due to arrive shortly to
transfer Koorland to Terra. In that time Laurentis had visited Koorland in the medi-cell to play regicide thirty-eight
times and Koorland had lost every single game. Laurentis
had offered to disengage his secondary processors during their latter matches but Koorland did not want any
such favours; a victory against an opponent that was not

trying their utmost to win was no victory at all. The captain grunted and moved a piece.

'That would be a succinct summary.' Laurentis' claw hovered above the board, digits clacking open and closed as he considered his next move. 'From our own experiences we can deduce as much, but combined with data from other observations made by the Adeptus Mechanicus vessels in attendance the evidence is utterly compelling. The orks have reached some new threshold of technological and societal expansion.'

'Orks have always had access to erratic but devastating tech – field projectors, energy beams and such. What makes the attack moons so different? One of their tech-savants has stumbled upon a gravitational disruption system.'

'If we encountered one, perhaps two of these battle stations I would agree,' said Laurentis. He moved a piece into an assassination position. Koorland frowned and studied the board with greater intensity. 'The manner in which this technology is widespread and the deployment of the attack moons in a pre-meditated manner, if not wholly efficient and co-ordinated, suggests a higher level of interaction.'

'Intelligent orks?'

'Orks have always been intelligent, captain,' said Laurentis. His artificial voice sounded strained, the modulators struggling to convey his disapproval. 'They have also been numerous and determined, a fact which in retrospect the authorities of our respective organisations have failed to consider over recent centuries.'

'The orks were broken by the Emperor at Ullanor,' said Koorland. He reached towards a piece, hesitated, withdrew his hand. 'There have only been scattered encounters for the last thousand years.'

'Which brings me back to my original premise. Only a madman, capable of an astounding and highly illogical leap of thought, could have predicted that the ork menace would return with such strength and means. From the records I have accessed, historical data concerning ork advancements is sporadic. However, I have discerned an underlying trend. Not a pattern, as one might think it, but a phenomenon. The orks operate in bursts of hyperactivity. They explode, rapidly expanding and showing technological advancement on an unprecedented scale, and then when defeated recede quickly. During the peak of their strength, their innovation and cultural intelligence is at its height.'

'They thrive on momentum.' Koorland knew that he was beaten and indicated as such before gently pushing away the board. 'Each conquest, every expansion, feeds into... whatever. Their orkishness?'

'Exactly. Aggression rewards and enables further aggression. Their progress is measured in plateaus swiftly reached, which may then decline in defeat or be sustained for a period until another major leap forward occurs.'

'The attack moons are one such leap?'

'Of the technological kind. Our companions in the Adeptus Astra Telepathica inform us that there has also been a psychic leap forward. The Beast, the driving force at the heart of the latest expansion, is an incarnation of ork psychic potential not seen before.'

'The two must be linked,' said Koorland, standing up. 'If

the Beast can be destroyed, the foundations of this current plateau of advancement will also be destroyed.'

Laurentis positioned himself in front of the Space Marine as Koorland stepped towards the chamber door.

'It appears that your heartbeat has increased, as have skin temperature, perspiration and other vascular activity. One might think that you are undergoing an adrenal rush prior to some form of action, captain.'

'I have just thought of something I must do.' Koorland stepped to the right but Laurentis shifted position to intercept him again. 'Step aside, or I will move you aside.'

'Indulge me for a moment, captain.'

'A moment.'

'The only reasonable explanation for your sudden activity is a resolution to act based on a conclusion drawn from our recent discussion. Reconsidering your words, it would also be logical to assume that this theoretical course of action is related to your conclusion that the ork advances might be halted by the removal of the Beast.'

'What of it?'

'The psychic and technological advances we have experienced are not the complete picture, captain. Biological and cultural advances are also highly likely.'

'What do you mean? That there are types of orks out there that we might not have encountered before?'

'Precisely, whether physically or relating to cultural role. The Beast, whatever it is, may be an ork of a different order to anything we have experienced. Increased psychic activity denotes a shift of parameters that eclipses any expectations we might already possess.'

'You don't think the Beast can be killed?'

'I am sure it can be eliminated. However, I am not sure that whatever plan of action you appear to be initiating will be capable of the feat.'

Koorland stepped back, rocked as if struck. Laurentis' cold declaration had hit him harder than a bolt-round, bringing home the realisation that the Imperial Fists were no more. Koorland steadied himself with a hand on the bulkhead, gripped by an emptiness he had never felt before.

'Apologies, captain, I meant no offence.'

'None taken,' said Koorland. He straightened up. 'Your assessment is right, magos. There's nothing I can do alone that would kill the Beast. And there are no more Imperial Fists for me to command in such an action.'

'Yet you have an alternative plan?'

'I do.' Koorland stepped towards the magos, forcing the machine-man to retreat quickly. 'I need to speak to an astropath.'

'A meeting I can facilitate, captain, if you would allow me.'

'Why would you help me?' said Koorland with a scowl.

'It is in the interest of all non-orks that the Beast is stopped. I know that you think me and my kind inhuman, Captain Koorland, but we do have the best interests of mankind in mind on occasion. The Adeptus Mechanicus can no more survive this current onslaught than the Imperium. If you have a plan that will counter the ork threat I am happy to assist.'

'Very well, lead on,' said Koorland, waving towards the door.

The two of them encountered only servitors as they made

their way aft and up to the top deck of the ship. Here two combat servitors were stationed at the archway that led into the astropath's crew quarters. The hulking creatures were bigger even than Koorland, with chainblades and gun barrels for fists.

Koorland was relieved when the two behemoths stepped aside at a clicked series of commands from Laurentis; the Space Marine was sure he could have bested the servitors, but it was better that he was able to avoid further confrontation with his Adeptus Mechanicus hosts. They were capable of rendering him comatose or immobile if they wished, and he had no desire to be held in such a way.

Following Laurentis, Koorland ducked under the arch and into the antechamber beyond. A bell chimed as they entered, alerting Astropath Daezen Asarain to their presence. Benches were arranged in a square looking at a dark stone sculpture depicting the Emperor as the messenger, one hand holding a star on an open palm, wings sprouting from His back. Laurentis and Koorland remained standing. Less than a minute had passed when one of the side doors swished open to reveal a surprisingly young-looking man in a dark green robe. His blank eyes regarded the two visitors as though he could still see. They widened in surprise.

'Captain Koorland! I was not expecting this honour.'

'I have a message to send.'

'Um, I am not sure...' Asarain's blind gaze strayed to Laurentis. 'That is, authorisation is...'

'I am giving authorisation,' said Laurentis as Asarain's voice trailed off. 'Please follow all instructions from Captain Koorland.'

'If you... As you say, magos.' Asarain looked back at Koorland. 'What sort of message, captain?'

'General broadcast.'

'Tricky, what with all of the greenskin roaring, and the death-screams are...' Asarain fell quiet as Koorland's brow creased into a deep frown. 'Of course, I will try my best, and we have relay stations to amplify the signal. I just felt you should know that communication is ever more precarious, what with us being located close to the heart of the ork psychic blanket.'

'The Beast is close?' said Koorland.

'Not the Beast, as such.' Asarain looked awkward, and wrung the tassel of his rope belt in his hands. 'There are all sorts of strange signals bouncing back and forth through the warp. The Beast, the roar of his coming, is strongest, but it is not the only one. Or it is, but it is echoing back from somewhere else. Or the Beast is echoing back all the other roars. It's complicated, and we're not quite sure on the mechanism. Basically, there's an awful lot of roaring.'

'Can you send the signal, yes or no?'

'Yes, I can send it.' Asarain nodded vehemently. 'If it's complicated, any subtleties and nuances might be lost. The reverberations of the ork outbursts mean that we must focus on a simple, strong pulse.'

'The message is very short. Just three words. I want you to broadcast them as hard and as far as you can. Every relay station, every astropath that hears it is to send it on. I need this signal to break through the ork noise and spread from one end of the Segmentum Solar to the other. Is that possible?'

'I will add a rebound cadence to the transmission so that it receives further general broadcast. Three words? No sounds? No images? Any cipher?'

'Just three words, as loud and clear as you can make them.'

'As you wish.' Asarain shrugged. 'The signal should penetrate the green fog without too much effort if that is the case. What are the words?'

Koorland took a deep breath and considered the consequences of his actions. Three words would put into motion a plan laid down by the great Rogal Dorn a millennium ago. Technically, what Koorland was about to do was treason – a gross breach of the oaths sworn after the Heresy War when Lord Guilliman's reforms were enacted. Koorland did not care. These were dire times. The Imperial Fists were destroyed, his honour already crushed. Fell times called for fell actions.

He fixed Asarain with a stare and uttered the three words.

'The Last Wall.'

SEVEN

Terra – the Imperial Palace

Of late, the Clanium Library looked less like a library and more like the command bridge of a starship, and not by coincidence. Lansung's 'strategic consultations' were carefully stage-managed affairs, choreographed to make the Lord High Admiral the centre of attention whilst giving the appearance that all of the other High Lords had equal input. Dressed in the full glory of his elaborate uniform, the tails of his dress coat tipped with golden skulls, breast veritably clanging with medals, Lansung cut a striking figure as he paced and pouted, strode and frowned his way through the consultations.

Nearly all of the shelves that had been stacked with books, flexi-discs, crystal data cells and digi-scrolls had been removed, replaced with chronometric displays, tri-d hololiths and quasi-spatial projectors operated by lexmechanics from the same temple as the Fabricator General. Nothing but the best, the Senatorum had been assured. No resource spared during this time of crisis.

It was a charade, of course. All real military decisions, those taken at the highest level, were agreed in advance between the aides of the Navy and Imperial Guard. Matters were far too complex, the logistical arrangements alone requiring thousands of Administratum staff, for discussion in open assembly. The willing participation of the other High Lords perplexed Vangorich. It was as if they reasoned that their own status was elevated by Lansung's grandiosity. Even those Vangorich had once thought entirely sensible, not as venal as the rest of the Senatorum, seemed consumed now by the desire to be shown to be in control. Having sacrificed their power to Lansung they now crowded close to him so that they might somehow gain a little of it back, reflected by his beneficence.

Some of the gains made by earlier alliances were clearer to see now. The Administratum had lost a proportion of their control of military materiel directly to a branch of the Imperial Guard. The newly instated Departmento Munitorum operated out of exactly the same wings and buildings of the Imperial Palace, but now under the stewardship of quartermaster-colonels and logistarius-majors. Clerks whose families had served the Administratum loyally for five generations or more were now nominally Guardsmen, much to the surprise of the tithe-counters and manifest assessors themselves.

Yet what was given in one hand was taken with another. All Imperial Guard regiments being raised to combat the ongoing crisis were required, by a vote of the Senatorum, to include a proportionate number of staff from the Adeptus Ministorum. Preachers for the most part, but also armed members of the Frateris Militia that served the Ecclesiarch, were now required to encourage and protect the faith of the men and women who would be laying down their lives against the ork menace.

It was the rise of these Frateris Militia – zealous worshippers of the God-Emperor led by fiery demagogues and manipulative cardinals, growing quickly in number – that indicated the price Ecclesiarch Mesring had wrung from Lansung and Lord Militant Verreault for his support.

And behind it all, the Adeptus Mechanicus were happy to watch the flow of wargear from their forge worlds increasing with each passing day, while the shipments of precious ores and labourers in return grew by equal measure.

It sickened Vangorich to see these men, and the organisations they represented, glutting themselves on the people of the Imperium. The very same citizens they were meant to be moving to protect were working harder, longer and in worse conditions to provide the arms – and the blood – to bolster the egos of those that now controlled the Senatorum. It not only offended his sense of service, but also his love of efficiency. The bloated Astra Militarum, Navy and Ecclesiarchy required an equally engorged Administratum.

In response to the ork threat it seemed as if the Imperium, at least the Segmentum Solar, was puffing itself up like some creature trying to scare off a predator. Not that any of this was making any measurable impression on the front line of the war, because the ships needed to convey these growing armies from their home worlds were all being drawn to Lepidus Prime or Terra itself.

The screens and displays showed the latest reports on the

ork advance – if the semi-random encroachments could be called such a thing – and the various Imperial responses to the emerging threats. It was all slightly nonsensical even without Lansung's theatrics. Even with the benefits of astrotelepathy, it took an average of two weeks for a message from the outer Segmentum Solar rim to reach Terra. Disturbingly, as the ork attacks had progressed, the typical delay had been reduced to a little over ten days. Even so, by the time a message arrived and a ship was despatched in response, and the report from that ship was received, a whole month might have passed, if not more.

Lansung had been explaining, in long-winded fashion, the latest fleet manoeuvres and despatches for thirty minutes and more. He was in full gush when a sharp crack of metal on wood interrupted proceedings.

All eyes turned to Wienand, who had struck the table in front of her with the base of a heavy goblet. Lansung frowned and turned to the Inquisitorial Representative. Vangorich affected indifference, but was intrigued to find out how Wienand was going to play her next move.

'Is there something amiss, Inquisitor Wienand?'

'There certainly is, Lord High Admiral,' Wienand replied as she stood up. 'It seems that events are proceeding more swiftly than you would have us believe.'

Lansung took umbrage at this accusation, his chins and cheeks wobbling with indignation.

'I assure you, Madam Inquisitor, that Naval Command is fully abreast of the current situation and responding as swiftly as required and possible.'

'Is that so?' Wienand strode past Lansung and whispered

something to one of the lexmechanics. One of the hololiths shifted focus, zooming in to the mustering zone at Lepidus Prime. 'For several weeks now you have been telling us how you are gathering a sizeable fleet at Lepidus Prime. A considerable part of the segmentum fleet, in fact.'

'That is true, Madam Wienand. What of it?'

'And the reason for this accumulation of Naval power is to launch a counter-offensive against the orks on several fronts?'

'That is so, as I have explained in detail previously.'

'You have informed us that likely targets will be Syani, Locrastes, Asgarand and other systems in that vicinity, securing worlds towards the segmentum rim to divide the ork mass.'

'That would appear to be the most likely route to victory as this time, yes. If you need me to reiterate any of the smaller details, to aid your understanding of these somewhat specialist matters, I could do so at your convenience. However, if you would allow me t–'

'Lord High Admiral.' Wienand's voice was as sharp as a Lucifer Black's glaive. 'Is it not true that the greater part of this fleet has recently left Lepidus Prime?'

Lansung looked at his aides, who met his glare with shaking heads and shrugs. 'I do not believe so, Madam Inquisitor. Their orders–'

'So there is not a large flotilla en route to Port Sanctus in the Vesperilles System?'

Vangorich hid a smile with a fake yawn as he watched Lansung flail for a moment. Just for a second Vangorich thought the admiral would be stupid enough to deny this fact, which would allow Wienand to ask if he was indeed in control of the fleet or not. It was obvious that Wienand was not asking idle questions, but had intelligence to back up her claim. Lansung recognised this before uttering any denial. He instead opted for silence while he considered his position.

'You are aware that Port Sanctus is currently an ork-held system, Lord High Admiral?'

'Of course,' replied Lansung, grateful to be on more sure footing. 'The shipyards there have managed to hold out against initial attacks, but they are sorely pressed.'

'So Admiral Acharya is proceeding on your orders to liberate the docks at Port Sanctus?'

'Acharya?'

The single word betrayed Lansung's utter ignorance of what had happened in Lepidus Prime. Vangorich could well imagine the whirl of thoughts going through the admiral's head. How did Wienand know before him? Why had Acharya set course for Port Sanctus? If the attack failed, would Lansung be blamed? If the attack succeeded, would Lansung be able to take credit?

These last two would weigh the most heavily, Vangorich guessed. He wasn't sure how Wienand had managed to set Acharya in motion, and he would dearly like to know, but regardless of her methods the inquisitor now had Lansung trapped between two unknowable outcomes. If Lansung denied any knowledge of these manoeuvres, to insure himself against future failure, he gave up the pretence of being in control. If he took credit for them he was setting his fate on a course over which he could not exercise any control from Terra.

'It seems my orders have reached the fleet earlier than I had expected,' Lansung said after a few seconds – seconds that must have felt like hours to the cornered admiral. 'I will be leaving shortly to take personal command of the attack at Port Sanctus. I was going to end today's session with this announcement, of course, but you have somewhat spoilt my surprise.'

'Surprise? I am sure the Senatorum does not like surprises, Admiral Lansung.'

'An over-indulgence, perhaps. I have been a little carried away by the exciting prospect of action at last. Yes, I can announce that the true fight against the orks will commence upon my arrival. With Port Sanctus secured as a forward base once more, the offensive we have been discussing in recent conclaves will be able to proceed immediately.'

Some of the High Lords greeted this news with claps, others were still confused, trying to catch up on everything that had developed over the course of the preceding minutes. A murmur broke out as the Ecclesiarch turned to his neighbours to loudly ask what was happening, while Lord Commander Militant Verreault limped out of the chamber shaking his head, trailed by officers and orderlies who glanced angrily back at their Naval counterparts.

Lansung was forced to stand in front of them all, smiling stupidly.

'Bravo!' cried Vangorich, standing up. He met Wienand's gaze for a moment and she allowed a twitch of a smile, acknowledging that that word of praise was directed at her. 'Victory cannot be far off now.'

EIGHT

Nestrum – Mandeville point

There was a slight increase in pressure as the airlock sealed, cutting off the landing bay from the chamber where Koorland and Laurentis looked back through the window at the departing shuttle. The inner door opened with a hiss, revealing a sharply uniformed Naval officer and two lines of armsmen with shotguns held in salute across their chests, their faces hidden behind silvered anti-dazzle visors.

'Lieutenant Greydove, at your service.' The officer clicked his heels and nodded his head. His hair was an unruly mane of blond, and a moustache of the same drooped past his chin. Almost as tall as Koorland but far more slender, the lieutenant moved with easy grace as he stepped back and gestured for the Space Marine and tech-priest to exit the airlock. 'Welcome aboard the *Achilles*.'

'Greydove?' said Koorland as he stepped into the corridor. Fully armoured, he filled the main passage of the small patrol ship. At a bark from their sergeant the armsmen slapped hands to shotguns and turned to create a column on either side of the arrivals.

'I'm from Ranesmud II, it's something of a traditional name there,' explained the ship's commander. He noticed Laurentis turning the other way, heading aft. 'Um, excuse me, magos, but your quarters are this way.'

Laurentis did not stop or turn around, but the remnants of his head swivelled on his neck-bracing to face the lieutenant with a battery of sensor lenses and one unblinking human eye.

'I wish to make inspections of this vessel's warp engine systems and plasma reactor. Captain Koorland is an exceptionally valuable asset that cannot be endangered by any oversight of maintenance or execution.'

'I assure you that my tech-priest, Kahibar, is highly c–'

'Your ship is too small to qualify for a tech-priest of magos level and attendant support servitors, therefore I am superior in respect of your current enginseer. Do not feel any insult on his account, he will understand the situation.'

'I insisted,' Koorland said quietly. This argument seemed to forestall any of the lieutenant's objections and Greydove visibly wilted.

'Very well, I hope that all is in order, Captain Koorland.' Greydove rallied, falling back on an overly stiff and formal tone to bolster his confidence. 'I shall convey you to your quarters.'

'The bridge, if you please, lieutenant,' said Koorland. The Space Marine started walking towards the prow, forcing Greydove to jog to keep up despite the officer's long legs.

'I, er, that is, the bridge is for Naval officers only,' Greydove said. 'Standing regulations, I'm afraid.'

Koorland stopped and Greydove almost ran into the Space Marine. The armsmen came to a halt around them, bumping into each other in a clatter of carapace-armoured breastplates and vambraces. The Imperial Fist carefully placed a hand on Greydove's shoulder.

'I asked out of politeness,' said Koorland. 'Do not make me insist.'

Greydove looked into Koorland's eyes, perhaps seeking some hint of compromise or sympathy. His gaze met two grey points as uncaring and sharp as pieces of flint.

'I see.' Greydove glanced at the men around him. Any authority he might have hoped to keep was quickly evaporating like the sweat that now moistened his brow. He swallowed and drew himself up to his full height – impressive against the armsmen but ineffective when compared with Koorland's bulk. 'As commanding officer I extend an invitation to you to accompany me to the bridge.'

'Good. I am happy to accept your invitation.'

Greydove dithered for a moment, shifting from one foot to the other.

'Honour guard, dismiss!' he barked, catching the sergeant of the armsmen by surprise.

'Sir?'

'You heard the command, sergeant,' Greydove said evenly. 'I am sure Captain Koorland does not need a gaggle of armsmen following him around at every turn.'

'Yessir!' snapped the sergeant. He called his men to offer

honours once more before they turned on their heels and marched back the way they had come.

'I would appreciate it, captain,' said Greydove when they were out of earshot, showing genuine anger, 'if you would at least pretend that I am still in command of my own ship. Once you have been taken to the Sol System and departed I must still maintain discipline. You are undermining my authority. My orders permit me to restrain you if necessary, but that would be inadvisable for both of us, wouldn't it?'

'It would,' said Koorland. He bowed his head to acknowledge the lieutenant's request. 'Apologies for any problems my behaviour may have caused.'

Mollified, Greydove once again clicked his heels and nodded in salute. He turned and led Koorland along the main passageway of the ship, two hundred feet to a set of steps that led up to a pair of hydraulically-locked doors. Two armsmen flanked the portal, which wheezed open at a word from one of them.

Koorland followed Greydove inside. He noted two other officers – one manning the communications panel and another standing beside what appeared to be the sensor and weapons controls. A row of small screens flickered at waist height and altogether the bridge felt cramped, in marked contrast to the Chapter vessels on which Koorland had travelled for most of his life. The Space Marine stooped slightly to avoid banging his head on the pipework and girders that criss-crossed the ceiling.

'Sir, I've been getting complaints from...' The communications ensign fell silent as he noticed the armoured giant now standing in the middle of the command platform. The young officer self-consciously cleared his throat and continued. 'Enginseer Kahibar is complaining about a surprise inspection, commander. I have no idea what he is talking about.'

'Sir, we are registering an acceleration in the warp engine conduits,' said the other officer before Greydove could respond to the first. 'It looks as though our warp engines are coming on-line.'

'I gave no such order,' said Greydove.

'That would be Magos Laurentis, I believe.' Koorland's voice sounded loud and flat in the close confines. He looked at the sensor ensign. 'What range to the departing Adeptus Mechanicus vessel?'

'Twenty thousand miles and increasing,' the ensign replied automatically, responding to the raw authority of the Space Marine captain. The Naval officer glanced at Greydove for reassurance. 'Um, commander, we received no signal to prepare for warp jump yet.'

'Lieutenant Greydove, please have your Navigator report to the bridge,' Koorland said quietly, standing beside the ship's captain.

'Why would I do that?'

'Because you have a change of orders, commander,' Koorland said.

The shrill whine of a warning siren cut off the lieutenant's response as red lights flashed across the bridge.

'Sir! Warp engines engaged!'

'Thirty seconds to translation,' barked a servitor just in front of Koorland and Greydove.

'What upon the Throne is that damned tech-priest doing?' the ship's commander demanded, turning on Koorland.

'A change of plans, commander. I am taking command of your ship.'

'You can't do that!'

'I already have. Magos Laurentis is activating the warp drive and I am currently standing on the bridge giving the orders. Which part of this scenario suggests to you, lieutenant, that I am not in complete control of the situation?'

Greydove opened his mouth dumbly a couple of times, searching for an answer. A desperate look creased his face.

'Don't make me assemble the armsmen, captain,' the lieutenant said, trying to sound stern.

'I will not think twice about killing your men,' Koorland said, uttering the words deliberately and slowly so that he would not be misunderstood. 'There is some chance that your men may succeed in pacifying me sufficiently for my return to Terra. They will not be able to do so without significant casualties.'

The Space Marine tried to reassure Greydove, taking the lieutenant's arm in a gentle grip.

'I intend no harm to this vessel or its crew.' Koorland straightened but did not turn as he heard the distinctive snick of a holster being unfastened. He looked Greydove in the eye. 'Tell your ensign to secure his pistol, otherwise I will be forced to take it from him.'

Koorland heard an exhalation, saw a slight nod from Greydove and then using the dim reflection on one of the communication screens watched the officer fasten the holster once more. 'Good. We should avoid any rash actions at this moment.'

'Translation in five seconds,' warned the servitor monitoring the warp drive. 'Four... Three... Two... One...'

There was a lurch inside Koorland as reality and unreality momentarily occupied the same space. Every atom of his being fizzed for a few seconds and in the depths of his mind, somewhere near the base of his brain, a disturbing pressure forced its way into his thoughts.

After ten seconds, the sensation had passed.

'Translation successful,' the servitor announced, rather unnecessarily. Had translation not been successful everybody aboard would know about it – or be dead.

'I– I take it that you are not intending to travel to Terra?' said Greydove.

'That would be a waste of time, lieutenant. The Imperium is under threat and a suitable response is required. Honour demands that I continue the battle. I intend to rendezvous with my remaining brothers.'

'I don't understand. I was led to believe,' Greydove dropped his voice to a whisper and glanced cautiously at the other men, 'in greatest secrecy, that you were the last warrior of the Imperial Fists.'

'We call it the Last Wall protocol. In the event that Terra should be under grave threat, perhaps even fallen, the sons of Dorn will come together to deal with the matter as one.'

'But, excuse the question, if you are all dead, who is there to respond?'

'The Imperial Fists Chapter may have been destroyed, but the old Legion will remember.'

'The old Legion?' Greydove was horrified by the concept. 'But the Legions were broken apart by decree of the Emperor.'

'Not the Emperor,' snapped Koorland, more harshly than he had intended. He took a breath. 'By Imperial decree, yes, but it was not from the lips of the Emperor that the decree came. It matters not. The signal has been sent and I will wait for those who are fit to respond.'

'But if you are not going to Terra, where are we heading?'

'The last place our enemies would look for us. A place that lives long in the memory of the Legion. Tell your Navigator to chart a course for the Phall System.'

NINE

Port Sanctus – Vesperilles System

After giving the order to translate, Rafal Kulik muttered a few lines of a prayer to the Emperor. He hated this moment, always had. Ever since his first voyage aboard the *Furious Pilgrim* and that fateful warp jump from Elixis, the process of translating had filled him with a physical sickness and an existential dread.

At least he no longer threw up with each transition. That had been cured by an old recipe from one of the gun captains aboard the *Invulnerable Faith*, who had taken pity on a poorly young fourth lieutenant he had found evacuating his stomach in the solitude behind the plasma relay dampers. The remnants of an ash-and-ginger biscuit were still sitting in Kulik's pocket, just in case of a resurgence of the ancient nemesis of nausea.

'Dear Emperor, please ensure that my ship survives this unnatural voyage, that my crew are delivered from the grip of the warp, and that my soul carries with me into the world of my mother,' whispered Kulik.

Shaffenbeck was about twenty feet away, ostensibly to keep an eye on the junior officers, but Kulik caught the occasional glance in his direction too. The rest of the watch crew on the bridge knew well enough to give their commander adequate space at this delicate moment.

For his part, Kulik was applying all the will he had not to stare at the transition countdown display, and occupied himself with an intimate inspection of the curlicued decoration of his sword hilt. Meanwhile the depths of his guts churned in anticipation of the shrieking wail of a siren that would warn of a Geller field failure or warp engine malfunction.

Sweat was wetting his over-starched shirt and the soles of his feet were itching – a sure sign that something was going to go wrong.

He barely heard the servitor's drone conclude the countdown. One moment Kulik was on the bridge of his ship, studying the lines of the basket hilt of his sword, the next moment he was adrift on the void of space, his soul bared to the flare of a billion angry suns, scorching his being from the inside out.

And then they were back in realspace.

Kulik took a long, deep breath, nostrils flaring and eyes wide like a charging bull as he fought back the somersault in his stomach with raw willpower. His hands were balled fists at his side, fingernails digging into flesh.

Finally, the captain let out an explosive breath.

'Full scan, cycle plasma coils, navigational shields to full power, void shield generators to maximum, targeting grids on full lock. All stations remain at battle readiness!'

The orders were the same every time, issued without effort or thought. Similarly, the watch officers on the bridge, and no doubt the warrant and petty officers in the bowels of the *Colossus*, were acting even before the words left Kulik's lips. They had been through the actions enough times on the long rimward patrols that they knew the post-translation drill by heart.

There was a slight cough from Lieutenant Shaffenbeck, and when Kulik looked at his second, the lieutenant shot a glance towards the doors of the bridge. There was another command not so familiar.

'Oh, and please extend my invitation to Admiral Price to join me on the bridge,' Kulik added.

As sensor vanes gathered data on the surrounding system, matriculation servitors analysed the information and cross-referenced with their memory stores of the surrounding star field. Saul double-checked the calculations of the lieutenant at helm control – Mathews – and nodded with satisfaction.

'Confirmed, Vesperilles System. Seventy thousand miles inside the Mandeville point, heading oh-oh-five-seven, inclination thirty-eight.'

'Captain!' The sharp call came down from Ensign Daggan assisting Lieutenant Sturmfel at the sensor banks on the level above Kulik. 'Reading multiple radiation sources, plasma discharge and other ordnance resonance.'

'Evidence of an engagement,' said Kulik, striding over to the scanner displays. 'Boost power, we need more clarity on the full-spectrum scan. Comms, broadcast identifiers and scan battle frequencies.'

Over the following minutes the situation became clearer. Sensor traces showed battle debris and munitions detonations ranging from several hours old to ten days. Residual warp backwash located more than fifty vessels already in-system, but scattered all around the perimeter as they had dropped out of warp space. A cluster of signals almost at right angles to the *Colossus*' position on the system plane showed where Admiral Acharya's fleet was gathering.

The orks were even more numerous. Scores of escort-size and dozens of cruiser-class and larger ships flooded the system, operating in small battlegroups that were targeting the isolated Navy ships attempting to reach the converging fleet.

'Sir, we have an Imperial ship under attack to port,' announced Lieutenant Sturmfel. 'Cruiser-class, three ork attack ships converging on their position. Read void shield overloads and superstructure damage. Radiation blossom indicates two destroyed ork ships in the vicinity.'

Kulik watched as the relative positions of the ships were plotted on a sub-display while the main screen continued to fill out with system details – planetary positions, gas clouds, asteroid belts and fields, and the scattered dispositions of both Imperial Navy and greenskin vessels. There was a line of more than thirty red enemy sigils between the *Colossus* and the flag rune depicting Admiral Acharya aboard the *Defiant Monarch*.

'Helm, come to new heading, nine-five-three, then all speed ahead,' announced Kulik.

'It's the *Saint Fatidicus*, captain,' said Shaffenbeck, moving away from the communications console. 'Captain Havaart is issuing an all-channels request for assistance.'

'Tell him we're on our way,' said Kulik.

The doors growled open to allow Admiral Price to enter. He ran a quick, experienced eye over the screens and then turned to Kulik.

'You intend to assist the *Saint Fatidicus*?'

'Aye, sir,' said Kulik. The captain paused, waiting to see if Price would overrule the decision. An admiral had no authority to countermand a ship's captain in the running of his vessel, but he could issue orders to that captain to engage or break away if his vessel was not in immediate danger.

'Very good. Carry on, Captain Kulik,' said Price, his voice quiet, the tone formal as befitted a combat situation.

Kulik nodded and returned his attention to Shaffenbeck.

'Request that Captain Havaart come to starboard by fifty points, if he is able. On our current course that will ensure that the two ork ships are between the *Colossus* and the *Saint Fatidicus*.'

'He'll be showing his arse to the third ork ship,' said Price.

Kulik darted a glance at the admiral, who held up his hands to admit he had overstepped his mark. 'Apologies, captain, please engage as you see fit.'

'Saul?'

'Captain Havaart sends an acknowledgement, sir.'

'The *Saint Fatidicus* is burning retro-thrusters and coming to a new heading, captain,' reported Daggan. 'Flanking ork attack ships are manoeuvring to intercept.'

Surprised, Kulik turned his gaze to the tactical display. As the ensign had reported, the two ork ships to starboard of the *Saint Fatidicus* had altered course not to head directly to the cruiser's new course, but to overhaul the ship and attack from ahead.

'That's odd,' he said out loud. Shaffenbeck came up to stand at the captain's left.

'Aye, captain. That's not usual ork behaviour, sir,' said the lieutenant. 'Normally they would just head directly for their target.'

'Yes, but what's even stranger is that their current course will take them into the arc of the cruiser's torpedoes. If they're smart enough to attempt an overhaul, why can't they see that they'll be disadvantaged by it?'

The two officers fell silent as they contemplated the problem. Ensign Daggan hesitantly provided the answer.

'Sir, they think that we have torpedoes too. On our current heading the *Saint Fatidicus* will be beyond the ork attack ships, meaning we cannot fire torpedoes without risking the other ship.'

'Emperor's Throne,' muttered Shaffenbeck, as much out of appreciation as surprise.

'Don't blaspheme,' Kulik replied automatically. He examined the display and saw that Daggan was correct. 'That would be a wonderful plan, but we don't have torpedoes, do we? Let's make sure these greenskins pay for the mistake.'

'Pretty sophisticated thinking for a bunch of green-arsed savages, isn't it?' said Price, joining Kulik and Shaffenbeck at the command centre of the bridge. The admiral had a frown of concern. 'There were reports that the orks were acting in a more coordinated fashion than we've become accustomed to, but I don't think I really appreciated what that meant until right now. If they've discovered fleet tactics more advanced than simply charging full throttle and firing off everything they have, we could be in for even more of a fight here than I expected. The attack moon is going to be difficult enough; a properly organised fleet defence could make our mission here impossible.'

Kulik looked at Price, surprised by the admission. The admiral looked genuinely worried, something Kulik had never seen before.

'It would seem that Admiral Acharya was guilty of a similar underestimation, sir,' said Shaffenbeck, indicating the Imperial fleet bottled up at the edge of the system. 'I expect he was hoping to make far more inward progress by this stage, perhaps even catch the orks unawares.'

'One thing at a time, Saul,' said Kulik. 'We'll help the *Saint Fatidicus* first and we can worry about the fleet situation later.'

'You mean I can worry about it,' said Price. 'I know you've got used to commanding the patrol flotilla, but this is my fleet, remember?'

'Aye, sir, of course,' said Kulik, accepting the criticism with a slight nod of the head. 'I did not mean to imply otherwise.'

'Of course not,' said Price.

The *Colossus* powered towards the other Imperial ship while the *Saint Fatidicus* turned towards them. As Price had predicted, one of the ork attack ships fell in behind the cruiser, directly aft where none of the Imperial vessel's weapons could be brought to bear. Shell detonations and sporadic blasts of laser fire rippled along the cruiser, exploding in flares of purple and blue against the void shields. It would be a rough ride for those aboard, Kulik was sure, but alone the ork ship didn't have enough firepower to breach the energy defences. Only when the other two ork ships came into range would the greenskins be able to punch through the void shields and inflict lasting damage.

'I had hoped that the two ships would come and take us on once they saw we were attacking,' Kulik confessed to Shaffenbeck. 'They don't stand a chance against a battleship, of course, but I've seen it happen before.'

'But these greenskins are too smart for that, sir,' said Shaffenbeck.

'Well we know that now, don't we?' Kulik shrugged, dismissing his annoyance. 'Havaart and his crew will have to weather a bit of rough treatment before we come into range.'

'Aye, sir, I'm sure it won't be anything they can't handle.'

Kulik could feel that *Colossus* wasn't proceeding quite as he intended. There was something about the vibrations through the deck, the background hum, that dissatisfied the captain. He looked at the course projection on the screen and saw that they had made minor alterations to their heading twice since he had laid down their course.

'Helm, can't you keep to a straight line?' barked Kulik, rounding on the navigational crew.

'Sorry, sir,' replied Lieutenant Asterax, whom Kulik had brought across to the *Colossus* when he had been made captain. Kulik expected better of his helmsman. 'There's a two point drift to starboard, captain.'

Kulik grunted to acknowledge the response and turned his attention to the Adeptus Mechanicus enginseer at the monitoring station on the upper level of the bridge.

'Fastandorin!' The captain's bellow brought the red-robed

tech-priest to the rail above. Her face was an articulated mask of silver and copper that showed no expression. An arterial cable spiralled away from her right temple to the cogitator behind her. 'There's a plasma flutter in the starboard engines. You have two minutes to stabilise it before I send Mister Shaffenbeck to take personal control.'

Every ranking man and woman aboard knew what that really meant. If Kulik despatched the first lieutenant to anybody's position, that officer would find themselves dumped dockside and on half-reparations at the next port of call. Kulik expected the best, and there were stories of unfortunates left abandoned on star bases and orbital stations deep in wilderness space who could not expect another Imperial vessel for many years, decades even.

'Analysing, captain,' replied the enginseer before disappearing from view. Her voice always reminded Kulik of something silky and smooth; beguiling and utterly at odds with her inhuman appearance. Fastandorin seemed oblivious to the effect it could have on the men around her, having devoted her life to matters of the machine above the flesh more than two centuries previously.

There was no need for a further report. Kulik could feel the dissonance that had niggled at him dissipating as the engine crews fixed the power imbalance. A few minutes later and there had been no further adjustments from the helm crew.

'Thank you, enginseer, please ensure such a situation does not arise again.'

'I will recalibrate the monitors myself, captain,' Fastandorin's reply drifted down.

The battleship was converging rapidly with *Saint Fatidicus*, with the ork ships approaching from behind and to starboard of the cruiser. As Daggan had predicted, the flanking ork vessels were between the two Imperial Navy ships.

'When is Mister Daggan due to sit his lieutenant's exam?' he asked Saul quietly.

'Next time we have any extended period at dock, sir,' replied Saul. 'It should have taken place at Lepidus Prime, but events overtook us before the board could be arranged.'

'Well, ensure that he goes forward next time,' insisted Kulik. 'And make sure he is thoroughly prepared. He's a good officer, Daggan, there's a ship somewhere that will benefit greatly from his promotion.'

'I understand, sir,' said Shaffenbeck, nodding. 'I will ensure he has my personal attention and tuition.'

'Very good.' Kulik raised his voice. 'Fire arrestors and slow to battle speed! All flight crews to launch stations. Divert power to lance batteries and weapons matrices. Pilots and gunners prepare for launch orders. Lieutenant Sturmfel, what is the current condition of the *Saint Fatidicus*?'

It was a few seconds before the sensor officer made his reports.

'Her engines are running hot, but void shields are intact, sir. No additional damage yet.'

'Very well. Lieutenant Shaffenbeck, launch all fighter and bomber wings as soon as we have attained combat velocity. Comms, signal Captain Havaart. When we have launched, he is to come about sharply and target the ship on his stern. We will engage the other ork vessels.'

'Aye aye, sir!'

In the flight decks pilots were warming up the plasma jets of their aircraft and ground crews were making last-minute checks on fitted ordnance and power feeds. Gun crews would be at their weapons, stripped to the waist, bare-footed to get grip on the rippled floor of the gun decks. The gun captains and deck lieutenant would be reminding the crews to await their orders, to mark the targeting matrices. Energy was surging though the coils feeding the lance turrets, charging the building-sized capacitors that would power the devastating laser weapons.

It was an illusion that Kulik thought he could feel the deceleration as the arrestor engines fired to reduce the battleship's speed, but the change in the throb along the deck under his feet was as much a signal as any report from the engine stations.

'Sir, ork ships are firing on the *Saint Fatidicus*,' rasped Sturmfel. He flicked a sweat-drooped fringe of dark hair out of his eyes. 'Extreme range, no hits yet.'

Kulik waited, affecting an air of calm, though inwardly he was counting down the seconds as the *Colossus* bled away enough momentum for the flight bays to disgorge their lethal cargo. Price moved closer, his presence a suddenly unfamiliar factor in an otherwise familiar environment.

'You have a bit of a flair for the dramatic, Rafal,' the admiral said conversationally. Any worry Price might have shown earlier had completely disappeared. He now seemed as relaxed as if they were on a touring schooner taking a pleasure trip into orbit, not about to engage in a deadly exchange of laser and shell.

'Sir?'

'Combat deceleration, emergency launches. You know, Captain Havaart could probably survive the extra couple of minutes it would have taken to perform a, let's say, more graceful entry into the combat sphere.'

'Starboard wings launching, sir,' announced Shaffenbeck before the bemused captain could reply. Then, a moment later, 'Port wings launching.'

'Lance arrays, target closest ork vessel. Attack wings are to engage second ork vessel. Helm, stand ready to come to port by twelve points, to bring starboard batteries to bear. Forward batteries, prepare to fire to starboard.'

Kulik's rattle of orders were relayed by the gunnery officers to the relevant crews. The captain crossed his arms and half-turned towards Price.

'Dramatic, sir?' Kulik's lips twitched with a smile.

'Positively theatrical, Rafal.' The admiral grinned and turned away. 'Not that it is any of my business, of course, captain. It is your ship.'

'Sir, *Saint Fatidicus* is under intense attack from all three ships.'

'On screen, now!'

The main display disappeared and become a swathe of black. A sparkle of light flittered in the top-left corner. As the image resolved and magnified, the glittering patch became a scene of the four ships. The Imperial cruiser seemed to be burning along one flank, but Kulik realised it was simply the arrestor thrusts turning the ship sharply around as he had ordered. From turrets along the spine of the ship bright white beams of lance shots cut and swerved across the ether. The whole ship was surrounded by a purplish miasma of discharging void shield energy.

The ork ship that had been on the cruiser's stern was a squat, blunt-nosed beast of a vessel, perhaps no more than five hundred yards long, but almost half as broad and high at the front. Ten, maybe twelve decks of guns and launchers bristled from its prow, massively front-heavy but capable of unleashing the equivalent firepower of a vessel many times its size. As the cruiser turned, the ork slid amidships on the port side. *Saint Fatidicus'* main broadside opened fire, engulfing the attack vessel with a welter of macro shell detonations even as the orks' forward batteries spat out a hail of missiles and shells. The greenskin ploughed through the onslaught of the cruiser, debris spilling from impacts all along its hull, while its own fusillade continued, burrowing through the void shields before smashing with terminal force into the buttressed hull of the *Saint Fatidicus*. Gun decks exploded outwards as magazines were penetrated by the brutish salvo, spitting men and jagged metal into the void.

Ahead of the *Colossus* the other two ork ships were turning away from the battleship, concentrating their fire on the prow of the cruiser. With the *Colossus* in its current position the cruiser could not launch its torpedoes. The battleship's forward guns were within range and suffered no such restriction.

'Open fire, all batteries.'

Targeting past the dozens of bombers and fighters now cutting a course toward the ork ships, the prow batteries lit up space with a pounding flurry of plasma shells and small-scale atomic warheads. They did not need to hit directly, the force of their detonations enough to cause the shields of the ork ship closest to the cruiser to flare bright orange, creating a stark silhouette of its bulbous, almost spherical hull.

'Re-targeting,' announced the gunnery commander. He was on the upper deck but his voice came through a speaker just in front of the command position where Kulik stood. 'Adjusting for range.'

'Ork ships are turning, captain,' came the report from the scanning consoles.

'Here they come,' whispered Shaffenbeck. 'Straight for us, I bet.'

'Belay fire order, check new course headings,' snapped Kulik. He didn't want to risk hitting the *Saint Fatidicus* if the orks drastically changed their heading.

'Sir, the orks are...' The lieutenant stopped and double-checked his screens. 'Captain, the orks are breaking away.'

'They're what?' Kulik's voice went up an octave with surprise.

'Disengaging, captain. New headings are taking them away from the *Colossus*.'

Kulik looked first at Shaffenbeck and then at Price. They were both as shocked as he was. It was the first lieutenant who voiced his surprise first.

'But surely that's premature? No ork would run from a fight without first at least firing a few salvos at us.'

'They must have known they couldn't win against a cruiser and battleship combined,' said Price. 'I'm surprised they didn't cut away sooner rather than take the risk.'

'Well, that's just it, isn't it, admiral,' said Kulik. 'They stayed long enough to inflict some damage on the *Saint Fatidicus* and then disengaged. Hit-and-run.'

'Do we recall air wings and pursue, captain?' asked Shaffenbeck.

Kulik looked at the sub-display that now contained the strategic system map. The orks were heading back towards a cluster of enemy signals around an asteroid field a few hundred thousand miles away. Only the enhanced sensor suites of an Oberon-class could distinguish between the dormant attack ships and the celestial debris. The captain's eyebrows rose even higher. 'Are they...? Are they trying to lure us into an ambush?'

'Emperor's Throne, that's subtle for an ork...'

'Don't blaspheme.'

TEN

Terra – the Imperial Palace

There was some satisfaction to be gained from knowing that matters were in hand and that plans long in maturing were finally bearing fruit, but Wienand knew better than to celebrate too soon. Though she sat in her quiet chambers with a sheaf of reports from Mars, Titan and the ships of the Battlefleet Solar, the Inquisitorial Representative's thoughts were fixed firmly on Terra. Lansung was, for the moment, en route to the front lines and incapable of solidifying his hold on the Senatorum. The fact remained that his influence had only been made possible by the self-serving nature of the High Lords currently occupying the Senatorum Imperialis.

A balance had been lost somewhere along the way. Wienand could not point to a particular period, a specific appointment, or name an individual responsible, but the checks and measures intended to keep the Senatorum functioning had failed.

Fixing it was just as complex, but Wienand had a plan now that Lansung was away fighting his war. The repairs had to begin from within the Senatorum Imperialis. To try to instigate massive changes from outside invited resistance and division, when unity was of paramount importance if the ork threat was to be dealt with.

However, there was an irony in that the very unity Wienand and others sought was the source of the current dysfunction. One of the regulating principles of the ruling council was that self-interest prevented the component organisations allowing any one or two of their fellows to gain too much power. A fractious harmony, tense but productive, was the best environment for government. Too many debates and nothing happened; too few and individuals like Lansung profited greatly.

The rot had started and would end with the Lord Commander. Udin Macht Udo and his predecessors could not be blamed for failing to live up to the standards set by Roboute Guilliman, but they should have been held accountable. It was the Lord Commander who sat as chair of the Senatorum and it was the Lord Commander who, by their title alone, was solely responsible for the protection and continuation of the Imperium. The Lord Commander could not have foreseen the ork resurgence but Udo certainly should have taken a lead in the response rather than deferring to Lansung. Whether corrupt or incompetent, Udo was no longer fit for the duty, but removing him threatened civil war.

A gentle knock at the door broke Wienand's train of thought. She realised that she had been subconsciously scribbling notes on the reports with her auto-quill even as her conscious mind had been examining the Senatorum issue. She sealed the papers back into the static-locked sleeve and called out for the visitor to enter.

It was Rendenstein, her latest attaché-cum-bodyguard. A former lieutenant in the Imperial Guard, she had been brought to Wienand's attention many years earlier and had submitted to months of physical and mental therapies to prepare her for a role as an inquisitor's agent. Rendenstein had aided her mistress in many investigations and proven herself invaluable in both fistfights and firefights. The secretariat had the demure appearance of a tall, well-proportioned middle-aged woman, but beneath her pale skin was a reinforced skeleton and bio-enhanced subdermic armour layer that made her extraordinarily strong, and able to withstand bullets and las-shots. Cerebral and secondary limbic processors gave her a reaction time impossible for a normal human.

Rendenstein was also capable of eidetic recall, due to the crystal storage device in her frontal cortex, making her ideal as a personal scribe, secretariat and assistant. She never forgot names, faces or dates.

'You have visitors.' There was no formality between the two of them. Rendenstein had quickly learnt that her mistress preferred accuracy and brevity over all other concerns. The two had saved each other's lives many times and though Wienand held the rank, they considered themselves equals with different skill-sets. The fact that they were occasional lovers sealed the bond between them. 'Lastan Neemagiun Veritus is requesting your attention.'

'Veritus is requesting? That does not sound like the Veritus I know.'

'Demanding. Sorry, I did not even know that he had arrived on Terra.'

'Neither did I, which means he intended to turn up unexpected on my doorstep. That also means he won't go away until I see him, so you might as well prepare a proper welcome and send him in.'

'He is not alone.'

'Oh? Let me guess...' Wienand considered who would be likely to accompany the veteran inquisitor. 'Samuellson? Van der Deckart? Asprion Machtannin?'

'Two of the three. Samuellson is not here, but Veritus has Namisi Najurita with him, and another I do not recognise.'

'Najurita? She is the last person I thought would find cause with Veritus. He and she could hardly be more different. All right, I will see them in the Octagon.'

'Should I remain with you? Is this a conclave?'

'Not yet, unless Veritus wants to make it official. I think I know what he wants, but let us find out from the man himself. But yes, I'll want you present to record everything. Just in case.'

After Rendenstein had left, Wienand locked away her reports and then slid the file repository back into the wall, absentmindedly shutting the concealing panel as her thoughts turned to Veritus. There was no point keeping him waiting; it would only shorten his temper even further.

She found her fellow inquisitors waiting for her in the Octagon as she had instructed. If ever the Inquisition was accused of being paranoid, the Octagon would be cited in evidence for the prosecution. The eight-sided chamber had the appearance of a reading room or antechamber, about a hundred foot across, lined with wood panelling. It was built on three tiers, with cushioned seats between the eight sets of steps leading to the lower floor. This lowest level betrayed some of the hidden precautions of the Octagon; the white stone was inlaid with lines of lead in a complex hexagrammic ward. Behind the wooden panels on the walls was a similar labyrinth of anti-psychic sigils and designs, powering a null generator that suppressed the abilities of any psyker within the room.

Such precautions were taken, it was claimed, to ensure that inquisitorial conclaves could be held in the Octagon without favouring one participant over another. Those with telepathic abilities would not be able to glean any advantage from their talent, nor unduly influence other members of the conclave.

This being the Inquisition, it was well understood but never stated outright that the wards also prevented psychic events of a more pyrokinetic, bio-electrical or otherwise outright hostile nature. It was an internally known fact that members of the Inquisition had sometimes – rarely and regrettably, they would say – disagreed so fundamentally with each other that such conflict was eventually resolved through physical combat. Conclaves were meant to avoid these situations by giving parties equal chance to voice grievance, philosophy and defence, and refer such argument to an ostensibly objective authority in the form of fellow uninvolved inquisitors. The Octagon was proof that such conclaves, bringing together inquisitors of opposite but equally passionately-held beliefs and politics, sometimes acted as a catalyst rather than a cure.

As the current Inquisitorial Representative Wienand had a slight advantage over her guests, in that she was able to observe them for a few moments on the screen hidden behind a panel beside one of the entrances, via a link to the concealed digi-recording systems of the Octagon.

Veritus was easy to identify, though Wienand had never met him in person. The ageing inquisitor wore a full suit of powered armour – even here in the heart of the Palace of Terra – painted white and adorned with much gilded ornamentation. Eagles, skulls and other Imperial insignia almost covered the plates. Veritus' head was showing: deeply lined, the signs of surgical scars on his bald scalp, skin hanging from his chin and throat like the wattle of some domestic fowl.

He was gesturing vehemently towards a slender woman sat on the upper tier of seats. She was almost as old as Veritus, grey hair pulled back tight and styled in an elaborate knot. She wore a coat of heavy black fabric, much like a military greatcoat with wide lapels and golden buttons, and baggy blue trousers tucked into black calf-boots. Namisi Najurita could have been some high-ranking Navy or Guard officer, were it not for the lack of medals and rank insignia. From what Wienand knew of her, Najurita's philosophy was one of working with and within the other Imperial organisations, at odds with Veritus' creed that the Inquisition was a distinct and greater power of the Imperium.

The younger man sat below Najurita was known to Wienand. Van der Deckart wore an adept's robe of dark grey, though a silver bodysuit glittered beneath the drab folds. He had been brought into the Inquisition by Veritus two decades before, and although he had since carved his own furrow he was always ready to support his former master when called upon. His hair was cropped tight, as was his beard, and he had an eagle tattoo covering his right cheek.

She had met Audten van der Deckart a few years earlier at Cenaphus Priam, before she had answered the call to come to Terra. They had both been investigating a merchant cabal suspected of siphoning away Imperial resources to local pirates. Van der Deckart had been poised to bring in the Imperial Navy and a contingent of Space Marines from the Inceptors Chapter. Wienand had informed Cenaphus Priam's Imperial Commander instead, who took swift action with local forces and the Adeptus Arbites to bring the merchant guild to account, much to Van der Deckart's embarrassment. She suspected his appearance here to be as much about that grudge as the ongoing politics of the Inquisition.

Then there was Asprion Machtannin. He was an oddly androgynous individual, with indistinct features, shoulder-length white hair and a slender build. His eyes were a startling blue and Wienand suspected his appearance was due to past experiments with the body-altering substance polymorphine. Certainly Machtannin's pale flesh had a clay-like quality. His dress was styled as often seen amongst the Imperial nobility, particularly uphive families of the inner Segmentum Solar: buckled boots, tight grey breeches, short red jacket with flared shoulders.

The last of Wienand's visitors was a woman who looked about the same age as the Inquisitorial Representative, with long blonde hair, a flat moon-like face, and dark eyes. Like

Van der Deckart she wore heavy robes, and by the way she sat away from the others out of deference and kept glancing at him Wienand assumed she was likely Van der Deckart's apprentice, or was until recently.

Though Wienand was tempted to make them wait a little longer, just to remind them that they had interrupted her duties, she decided that delaying the encounter was not worth the brief satisfaction.

With Rendenstein on her heel, Wienand entered the Octagon. Immediately she was the centre of attention, all eyes drawn to her as she nodded in greeting and made her way slowly down the steps to the bottom level where Veritus was waiting.

Wienand made every effort to keep her composure. One inquisitor carried the full authority of the Emperor and could, in theory at least, command the entire resources of the Imperium. Here were five inquisitors, a gathering that would give even an Adeptus Astartes Chapter Master pause. Wienand was well aware of how tenuous her position was and it was hard not to be intimidated.

She rallied her thoughts, rebounding from the implied threat with a determination not to be cajoled by this show of influence by Veritus.

'Lord Veritus, you honour me with your attendance,' Wienand started smoothly.

Veritus smiled, an unpleasant grimace that showed neither humour nor pleasure. The expression quickly became a sneer.

'Save your silken words for the senators accustomed to hearing them,' said the veteran inquisitor. 'I shall show everyone present the respect they deserve by cutting to the chase. You, Inquisitor Wienand, have been Inquisitorial Representative too long. Your proximity to the Senatorum Imperialis has clouded your judgement and corrupted your principles. In short, you have become as bad as those you are supposed to supervise. I am here to have you replaced.'

This was no surprise to Wienand, and she decided to match Veritus' forthrightness with her own.

'And you have no business interfering in this matter, Lord Veritus. I assume, by the fact that you have brought a quorum with you, that you intend to call a conclave on this matter. I ask you to reconsider. The coming of the Beast is a terrible threat to the Imperium we have all sworn to protect. The Senatorum Imperialis may have its faults, but stability is needed now more than anything. Do nothing rash or we shall see the Imperium split apart from within, and consumed from without.'

'As you seem to have forgotten, the Beast is not the only threat to the Imperium. There are subtler, darker powers at work that will exploit this situation. It was laxity that spawned this orkish horde, and further laxity may allow threats even graver to gain strength. If you wish to avoid undue upheaval, Wienand, there is a simple solution. Step aside from your position and the transition will be painless for all concerned.'

'Easier for you, yet still disruptive to the smooth running of the Senatorum.'

'The Senatorum understands that you are merely a token, a representative with only temporary authority to speak on behalf of the Inquisition. Besides, its smooth running is not my concern, merely its correct implementation of the Emperor's wishes.'

'To know a thing and to understand its ramifications are different matters, Lord Veritus. I am a known quantity – or so I allow the High Lords to believe.'

'And that is the problem, Wienand. The Senatorum are too comfortable. It is time that they are reminded the Inquisition is not their ally, nor their political tool. An inquisitor is the Emperor's gaze, the eagle that seeks out its prey without pity or bias.' Veritus paused for a moment and looked at the other inquisitors. 'I have no doubt a conclave will find in my favour. Step aside now so that the matter can be resolved.'

Wienand gauged the others in the Octagon. Najurita was the only one who would hear Wienand's case with an objective, perhaps even sympathetic ear. Veritus had been clever to include her, giving any potential conclave a veneer of balance. It did not fool Wienand. She would be hounded until she was cornered and forced to come before the conclave, and then she would be stripped of her position in the Senatorum and despatched from Terra. Veritus was offering her a way out with more dignity intact.

'This is an important matter,' said Wienand, knowing that she had to buy time. The fact that Veritus was trying to get her to step aside was telling. On past form he would have simply called the conclave together without warning. Maybe he was not so sure of his position as he claimed, or feared Wienand would rally sufficient support around her to head off the conclave. It was an error on Veritus' part to state his intentions rather than present Wienand with a fait accompli. 'You cannot expect me to make a decision on a whim, when the future of the Imperium is so fraught with danger.'

'Of course not.' Najurita spoke before Veritus could reply and all turned towards her. She stood up and looked at each of them in turn, eyes narrowed. Wienand assumed that Najurita had now seen through whatever pretence Veritus had used to gain her cooperation and attendance. 'It is clear that there is much to be discussed. Lastan, I am sure we can grant Wienand a while longer to consider her position. I would very much like the opportunity to speak with you further regarding your intentions here.'

The words were softly spoken but there was sharp iron in Najurita's tone. Veritus held her gaze for a moment before breaking away, looking down at his feet in submission.

'As you say, Lady Namisi. Some time for reflection so that the truth will emerge.'

Your truth, thought Wienand, even as she bowed her head in acceptance of the proposal. And your truth will see the Senatorum Imperialis shattered and the Imperium brought to ruin. Over my dead body.

ELEVEN

Port Sanctus – outer system

'This...' There was actually spittle flying from the lips of Admiral Acharya, spraying onto the lens of the vid-link aboard the *Defiant Monarch*. The monochrome display flickered light from the wood panelling of the captain's comms chamber, abutting the main command deck. 'This is outrageous. Intolerable! The orks are massing and if we do not bring the fleets together one or the other of us will be destroyed!'

Face underlit by the screen, Price leaned forward in his chair, arms resting on his knees, hands clasped. Kulik could see the admiral's effort to keep calm in the whiteness of his knuckles.

'Which is why you must come to us, admiral. Elements of my fleet have been arriving over the last three days and are still arriving. If we try to break through the orks we will be leaving these ships to be destroyed piecemeal.'

Relaxing, Price slouched back. The screen went into a fuzzy static while the reply was transmitted. It would be a couple of minutes before the signal reached Acharya and his response was bounced back to the *Colossus*.

'Sir, while Admiral Acharya moving his fleet to our position would be the best course of action, doing nothing is certainly the worst,' said Kulik.

Price lazily spun to face the captain, who was sitting on the other end of a glass-topped oval table. A strategic display glowed beneath a scattering of translucent report sheets and pieces of paper. Three Naval regulations books were piled on one corner, tatters of parchment and plas-sheet marking various pages. Evidently Price had been looking for some precedent or rule that allowed him to assert command over the senior admiral; equally evidently, from their conversation, he had been unsuccessful.

The chain of command, even more so than in the Imperial Guard, was inviolate. A ship could spend anything from a few months to a decade away from port, and during that time the authority of its commander had to be absolute. If an Imperial Guard regiment turned on its officers it could do a lot of damage on the world it was on; if an Imperial Navy ship went rogue it could terrorise multiple star systems.

Though Acharya was senior by only a few months, it might as well have been centuries for all the difference it made in the eyes of the Articles of War. Price was under no obligation for his ship or fleet to obey any order issued by Acharya, but neither could he issue any command of his own.

Kulik realised that Price was looking at him intently.

'No, Rafal, doing nothing is not worse. Doing nothing allows us and the arriving ships to remain close enough to the Mandeville point to translate out of the system if sufficiently threatened. Acharya has stuck his head into the noose, I see no reason why we should follow.'

'You would abandon the coreward fleet, admiral?' Kulik was shocked. Price's calm manner at the prospect was even more chilling. 'Tens of thousands – no, hundreds of thousands – of lives?'

'And add our own to the tally for no reason?' snapped the admiral. Price lurched to his feet and strode towards Kulik, snatching reports from the table as he passed them. 'Emperor alone knows how they are doing it, but the orks are alert and responding quickly to any movements we make. That attempted ambush when we arrived is just the start of their cunning. Asteroid fields all across the system have been seeded with their rock forts, ready to launch missiles and torpedoes the moment a ship comes within range.'

Price tossed the handful of papers in front of Kulik and leaned forward with his fists on the table.

'Any ship or small group – *any* – that comes near the orks gets pounced upon. If the rimward fleet commits to Acharya's position, we are as good as hanging ourselves in front of the orks like the bait in a snare. I'm pretty damn sure that's what Acharya intends but isn't saying. As soon as we move closer and the orks come after us, he'll either attack them from behind or move the fleet out towards the Mandeville point for translation'

'But if the...' Kulik trailed off as the screen crackled into motion again with Acharya's reply. Price whipped round, arms crossed.

'You've seen the dispositions, Price! The orks will destroy one or the other of the flotillas and then turn on the surviving fleet. But they don't have the massed...' Acharya's desperate plea trailed off and the admiral turned his head away for a moment. When he returned his look to the vid-capture unit, there was an almost serene smile on his face. 'Never mind, Price. It seems that events are overtaking us, anyway. Emperor's grace be upon you.'

The screen went blank.

'What in the name of the Emperor did he mean by that?' demanded Price, rounding on Kulik as if the captain should know. Kulik shrugged.

The internal comm beeped and a light on a panel beside Kulik lit up green. The captain reached over and flicked the receive switch.

'What is it?'

'Captain, registering fresh translations at the system edge,' said Shaffenbeck.

'Yes, we've been doing that for the last three days. What of it?'

'A lot of translations, sir. Sensor team estimates it at nearly a dozen in the last five minutes. We also have confirmation of one of the identifiers.'

'A dozen ships? Who?'

'It's the *Autocephalax Eternal*, sir,' said the lieutenant.

'Lansung's flagship!' exclaimed Price. He moved Kulik aside to lean close to the comms pick-up. 'Have your communications team open up a command channel with the flagship, right now!'

'Aye aye, sir,' said Shaffenbeck. 'Captain, what are your orders for manoeuvre?'

'Remain on station, lieutenant,' said Kulik. He looked at

Price and received a confirmation. 'Repeat flag order to the rest of the fleet. Ships are to remain on station until further command.'

Kulik flicked off the intercom after receiving Shaffenbeck's assent. Price moved back to his chair and flopped down.

'What in all that is glorious on Terra is Lord High Admiral Lansung doing here?' the admiral asked nobody in particular, waving his arms helplessly. He half-turned and looked sharply at Kulik. 'You know he hates me, yes? If it wasn't for the fact that I'd already made post rank I'd have never become captain once he rose to power.'

'I have never heard the full story, sir. Something about a public disagreement.'

'That'll have to wait, Rafal. Find out where Lansung's flag-ship translated and plot a course. I expect the Lord High Admiral will want us to come calling on him.' Kulik gave Price a look that, whilst not openly disobeying a command from a superior, reminded that superior that he was captain of this ship, not some messenger ensign to be sent on errands. Price shrugged. 'No time for bruised sensibilities, Rafal. Sorry, but you'll just have to put up with me for the next few days until everything with Lansung and Acharya is smoothed out.'

'Aye, and I'll say thank you too, I'm sure,' Kulik muttered as he stood up.

'What was that, captain?'

Kulik stopped with one hand on the curved gilded handle of the wood-panelled door. He didn't look back.

'Aye aye, admiral. I'll get right on it.'

* * *

And for the next two days, that was exactly what Kulik did. Price's communications requests to the Lord High Admiral's flagship were repeatedly ignored or refused, leaving the admiral short-tempered and sarcastic; a mood Kulik had no desire to endure. Kulik inspected each gun deck and gun, every lance battery, both flight decks, the ship's shuttles and even the plasma core chambers in an effort to be wherever Price was not. In his absence Shaffenbeck, ever-patient Shaffenbeck, fielded any and all inquiries, requests and orders from the tetchy admiral, including the hourly demand for the comms officers to establish communication with the *Autocephalax Eternal*.

During this time the other ships of the fleet did relatively little. Acharya's coreward fleet maintained a defensive encirclement in orbit above the eighth planet, where it had been virtually trapped since punching in-system on arrival. The orks tried a few small attacks, perhaps hoping to bait the clustered Imperial vessels into a pursuit that would draw them out, but nobody was willing to break the relative sanctuary of the fleet.

The rimward fleet of Price maintained its own position just a few thousand miles from optimal translation distance, compact enough to defend itself but not so close that it could not disperse within a couple of hours to achieve translation separation. The newly arrived portions of Battlefleet Solar, eighteen more capital ships and twice that number of escorts, gathered on the system edge as they arrived, roughly equidistant between the two Naval flotillas.

They could not wait forever though, as the gigantic attack moon at the heart of the greenskin armada drifted ever closer to the docks at Port Sanctus. The orks were not to be distracted from their purpose by the presence of the humans, and their devastating weapon did not change course to meet the incoming fleets.

Under the guise of worrying about a visit from the Lord High Admiral, Kulik personally supervised gun practice and guard of honour drill. He instigated several new standing orders, including forbidding whistling and singing outside of crew quarters. Kulik individually briefed his officers on what to expect and do should Lansung decide to come aboard – all thirty-two lieutenants, flight lieutenants and ensigns. He was about to start going through the roster of sixty-eight petty and warrant officers, theoretically including the Navigators and tech-priests, when he received word from his first lieutenant that they had received fresh orders from Admiral Lansung.

Price received the ciphered communiqué in the comms chamber, with Kulik and Saul in attendance. However, before the admiral had entered his decipher codes the intercom buzzed with a message from the bridge. Saul took the transmission with the hand-held receiver, nodding and saying 'Yes' and 'Understood, lieutenant' every few seconds. After about half a minute he hung up and turned to find the captain and admiral staring inquisitively at him.

'Sensor report, sirs,' said Shaffenbeck. He cleared his throat. 'Lieutenant Chambers reports that the *Defiant Monarch* is breaking orbit and moving towards the system rim.'

'Acharya is leaving?' Price seemed torn between incredulity and delight.

'It would not be appropriate for me to venture speculation,

admiral,' Shaffenbeck said. 'Nor did the fourth lieutenant care to offer any such opinion.'

'Your orders, admiral? Perhaps they make mention of Acharya's departure,' said Kulik.

Price returned his gaze to the screen, still slightly euphoric if his distant smile and glazed expression were any indication. He keyed in a cipher code on the rune pad beneath the monitor and the display flared with static. After a few seconds, the fizzing monochrome resolved itself into the equine features of Admiral Sheridan Villiers, His Grace the Void Baron of Cypra Nubrea – Lansung's senior fleet attaché.

'For the attention of Admiral Price, Commander-in-office Rimward Flotilla, Fleet Navalis Segmentum Solar.' Kulik was mesmerised by the bobbing laryngeal protrusion of Villiers, which looked like an ork attack moon in its own right. 'You are hereby requested and required, immediately upon receiving these orders, to convene the rimward flotilla in accordance with the attached designations and dispositions, for preparation of immediate battle.'

The image halted, cut by flickering lines as Price paused the receiver. His expression had hardened at the words 'immediate battle'.

'Lansung intends to continue with this damn fool plan of Acharya's,' the admiral said without looking at his companions. 'He really means to liberate Port Sanctus.'

'Do you think that it was his intent all along, sir?' asked Shaffenbeck.

'But why send Acharya away now?' said Kulik. 'That doesn't make sense if he was acting on Lansung's orders.'

'We might never know, gentlemen,' said Price. He leaned forward and pressed the rune to continue the vid-flow.

'According to said dispositions, the rimward flotilla will make all speed to the co-ordinates indicated.' A series of nine numbers flashed up at the bottom of the transmission, somewhere within the orbit of the sixth world, Kulik judged on first glance. 'At the same time, the coreward flotilla shall perform counter-manoeuvres with effect to break through to the same position, linking the fleets. As an added measure, the Lord High Admiral shall be leading the Fleet Solar elements on a corresponding course to intercept any enemy vessels attempting to reinforce at the rendezvous.'

Price nodded, pausing the playback again.

'That's not a terrible plan,' the admiral admitted. 'Given our current positions, those headings will break the ork presence in two places, with Lansung's ships circling around to cut off the greenskins from the inner system where the attack moon is.'

'Aye, sir, but he hasn't taken into account the asteroid forts and other defences littered throughout that area,' said Saul.

'I think he has,' Kulik said quietly. 'He intends for us to clear that asteroid belt of the orks as we make our way to the rendezvous.'

'Attack the rock forts and then straight into a head-on battle?' Price frowned and leaned back in his chair to snatch a system-wide sensor report from the table. The creases in his brow deepened and the corners of his mouth descended even further. 'Bloody madman, that's what he is! I knew this was too simple.'

Kulik looked over the admiral's shoulder at the schematics to refresh his memory on the strategic situation.

'It is risky, sir, but it will place us in an ideal position to form up for an attack on the ork base,' said the captain. 'I really think Lansung intends to go for it as quickly as possible.'

'None of this makes sense,' complained Price, tossing the report back onto the table. He stabbed a finger at the playback rune and Sheridan Villiers' distorted face sprang into life.

'Stand ready to receive personal messages from the Lord High Admiral. For the eyes and ears of Admiral Price only.'

Kulik and Shaffenbeck both stepped towards the door but were halted by a wave from Price.

'I certainly don't care if you listen in,' said the admiral. 'If this is about Acharya it'll save me the bother of telling you myself.'

Villiers' elongated features disappeared, to be replaced by the bloated face of Lansung. It struck Kulik that the monitor controls had somehow malfunctioned, ballooning the one into the other. Lansung's cheeks wobbled and his chins rippled as he spoke.

'Listen here, Price. I know we have our history together, and I won't say that I've forgotten or forgiven. But that doesn't matter for the moment. That damned idiot Acharya has put the reputation of the Imperial Navy in jeopardy. Yes, I know what you're thinking – it's my reputation really, yes? Well, it's yours too, Price. I don't know why, or how, but someone got to Acharya and either persuaded him or forced him to make this attack. There's going to be hell to pay for him when this is over. He'll be lucky to command a garbage scow if he survives the judgement of the court martial he's got coming. Anyway, that's not of concern yet.'

Lansung shifted his bulk, moving further from the vid-capture unit. He splayed his hands across his chest, which bulged between the gaps in his buttoned coat.

'We can't afford to lose here, Price. It's not common knowledge, but the Imperial Fists took a pounding at Ardamantua. They were almost wiped out.'

Kulik heard Shaffenbeck gasp at this admission, and was shocked himself.

'We need a victory and damned quick if we want to salvage anything from the situation. Hate me all you like, but unless I return to Terra with a victory, and my authority intact, the whole Senatorum Imperialis is going to lose faith. And frankly, whether the other High Lords like it or not, this is a war that the Navy is going to have to win for them.

'Acharya was far off the mark when he brought the fleet here, and it's forced my hand. If we withdraw, our reputation will be worthless, and there's half a dozen admirals lined up behind me just waiting to pull away the steps and take my place. We do not need a power struggle in the upper echelons of the Imperial Navy at this time. You think I'm a ruthless career-minded pig. In fact, those were your exact words, I recall.'

Kulik watched Price out of the corner of his eye, but the admiral was intent on the screen, eyes fixed, expression unmoving.

'You are right, I probably am. But I am not a monster. Billions have died already trying to halt this greenskin tide. If we cannot hold them to a reverse now, all hope will be lost.

I don't care if we have to sacrifice the whole bloody segmentum fleet to win here, victory is the only option.'

The admiral wiped the sweat from his face with an embroidered handkerchief, which he stuffed up the sleeve of his coat.

'When we have the fleets together, then we can discuss options. Until then, I request and require that you follow my orders to the letter. Believe me, it is our best chance to get out of this mess alive and with honour intact. May the Emperor guard you in the dark places where you must fight, Admiral Price.'

The screen went black. Kulik blinked a couple of times, trying to process everything he had just heard.

'He didn't seem so...' Shaffenbeck let the thought drift away as Price turned a withering stare upon the lieutenant. 'Shutting up now, sir.'

'The fat oaf is right,' said Price, lip curled with distaste at the fact. 'Sooner or later we have to find out a way to destroy these moons, so we might as well start the job here. Damn Acharya, though, for going rogue. And damn Lansung for putting the bastard in charge of the coreward fleet in the first place.'

'What are your orders, sir?' asked Kulik, standing to attention.

'I don't know, yet. Decode the dispositions command and transmit to the flotilla. I'll look over everything else and give more specific orders of battle once we are under way.'

'So, we attack, sir?' asked Shaffenbeck.

'You heard the orders, lieutenant,' said Price. 'With immediate effect. Damn straight we're going to attack, and damn our souls if we let the coreward take the glory!'

TWELVE

Terra – the Imperial Palace

'Arrogant, like you said, sir,' said Esad Wire, better known to Vangorich as Beast Krule. 'Veritus has taken chambers in the Ecclesiarchy dorms on the Western Projection. Hardly any security at all. Thinks that being on Terra, being an inquisitor, makes him invulnerable. No doubt the Emperor will protect him. Van der Deckart and his interrogator, Laiksha Sindrapul is her name, they're a bit smarter. They've holed up in the Senatorum Rotunda until the conclave. There're more guards there than at the Ecclesiarchy holdings, but nothing that would present a problem.'

Vangorich held up a hand to stop his Assassin's report. Through the narrow window of his chamber – relinquished from the grasp of a lower overseer in the Administratum a few days earlier – the Grand Master looked over the turrets and roofs of the Imperial Palace's northern stretches. In particular his eye was drawn to the dozens of chimneys that sprouted from behind the crenellations that capped the Tower of Philo. Amongst the grey smog was a slightly darker smoke, reddish in colour. It was, Vangorich knew, caused by the burning of cachophite incense, and was the signal agreed with Wienand that the two of them should meet at the Sigillite's Retreat.

'In short, none of them are beyond easy reach?' Vangorich asked, standing up. Krule stepped to one side as the Grand Master headed towards the door. His hesitancy in replying caused Vangorich to stop and turn a suspicious eye on the Assassin. 'That is the case, is it not?'

'Machtannin has... gone missing, sir.'

Though his temper was tested, there was no point in Vangorich berating Krule for what had happened. They exited the chamber and entered the disused room beyond. A score of clerks had been moved to another wing following the relocation of their overseer, leaving rows of desks, each with illuminatorum screens and digi-quills still intact. A hexabacus had been left behind on one of the desks and there were a few personal belongings: prayer books and beads; an etchograph of a paternal-looking figure; a pair of fingerless gloves remarkable by their gaudily knitted pattern; other odds and ends of no import.

Old bare boards creaked underfoot as they passed between the empty work stations.

'And Hurashi of the Culexus has been informed?' Vangorich asked. 'She will be ready with an operative should we need it?'

'Yes, sir, the anti-psykers are ready for your word. Veritus' entourage seems to be mundane. Mostly ex-Guard and ex-Frateris as far as I can tell. Some augmetics and bionics, and quite an arsenal between them. The others have entourages with some muscle but mostly academic and administrative. According to Wienand's report only Najurita is a psyker, and isn't she on our side?'

'Nobody is on our side,' Vangorich said, more hastily than he had intended. He recovered his composure. 'Not even Wienand. We are each striving for our own agenda. Never forget that.'

'Of course. There is a rotating watch being kept on the others, sir. I'll be handling Wienand myself.'

'Good. Get some rest, your mark will be busy for the next hour at least, I would say. You'll be able to pick her up again in the sub-basement beneath the Ice Conservatory.' The knowledge that he had deduced the inquisitor's route to the Sigillite's Retreat gave Vangorich a satisfying warmth in his stomach. 'Be ready for anything.'

Krule nodded and broke away, heading out of a side door while Vangorich continued towards the end of the chamber. The Grand Master waited at the door for a moment, listening intently. There was no sound outside. He opened the door and stepped out into the empty corridor. Crossing the wide passage to a nondescript door opposite, Vangorich let himself into the dormitories for the former workers of the scriptorium he had just left. Bare wooden cots, small side tables and foot lockers were where their occupants had left them, though the bedclothes had been stripped. The walls were tiled with white, as was the floor, giving the bare room a clinical, sterilised feel.

Vangorich moved aside the bunk at the far end and carefully pulled out a broken wall tile near the floor to expose a keyhole. Kneeling, he slipped a key from his waistband and turned the lock. Part of the wall shifted fractionally into the room. Shuffling back, Vangorich used the key as a handle to lift the hinged portal, exposing the foot of a ladder disappearing below the dormitory. Withdrawing his key, the Master of Assassins replaced the broken tile, ducked into the small alcove behind the wall and pulled the door shut behind him.

In gloom he descended the ladder, counting out ninety-three rungs. The ladder continued down all the way to the sub-levels, another seven hundred and eight steps; he had counted them himself. Still in total darkness he stepped out to the left, swinging himself out into what seemed like thin air. The tip of his boot scraped against a ledge no wider than his thumb while the fingertips of his left hand found a similar purchase just above head height.

He edged spider-like for ten feet, between what he had subsequently discovered were the walls of an Ecclesiarchy chapel and the robing rooms of the female clergy members. He wondered if the small hidden space into which he lowered himself had first been designed by a less-than-chaste preacher or cardinal. It mattered not; the small door that had once led to it from a trapdoor in the chapel had been blocked with ferrocrete.

From here, Vangorich was able to move, bent almost double, through the collapsed catacombs of the Shrine of Imperial Mercies, once the Palatine Tower that had guarded the inner western curtain wall of the Imperial Palace. Still without any light he counted the crab-like steps until he came to an empty tomb. Pulling aside the cover, he pulled himself into the sarcophagus.

Floorboards overhead turned into rafters, in a way only found in somewhere as labyrinthine as the Imperial Palace. Dropping down ten feet to a solid wooden floor, Vangorich straightened and dusted himself off. From here it was just a few feet to the rotating section of wall that left him looking through one of the archways leading to the Sigillite's Retreat.

Wienand was already waiting for him, as he suspected she would be. The ruddy smoke had been their agreed sign for urgent action. She was bent over a digi-scroll reader.

'Which one of them do you want dead first?' Vangorich asked, stepping into the bare garden.

Wienand sat up and her head snapped round in shock. She took a deep breath, shook her head in disapproval of Vangorich's theatrics, and stowed the scroll reader in a bag in her lap.

'None of them,' she said after a moment's thought. 'Tempting as it is, I don't think I want to go that far, and certainly not using one of your operatives. You do know that your department is only meant to act with the approval of the High Lords?'

'A technicality. The High Lords. A High Lord. Is there a difference? And, as a member of the Inquisition, you bear the Emperor's sigil. Your voice is His voice. The whole of the Imperium is yours to requisition, should you wish. You only need to ask...'

'It would still cause ripples. A tidal wave, in fact. Look, let's keep this brief. I came to warn you that Veritus is about to bring together the conclave to judge my actions as Inquisitorial Representative. Even if somehow I manage to wriggle out of that, I will be suspended from my office for the duration. I'm sure Veritus has someone already in mind should the Senatorum be convened in the meantime.'

'By which you mean that Veritus will ensure the Senatorum is convened in your absence and his man, or woman, will take your place as the Inquisitorial Representative?'

'Yes, exactly.'

Vangorich paced along one of the paths, avoiding the cracks between the slabs, to test himself rather than out of superstition.

'Which one will it be?' he asked.

'What do you mean?'

Vangorich stopped, pivoted on his toes and looked at Wienand, his hands on his hips.

'Which of Veritus' followers is going to be replacing you? I could, you know, have them made unavailable.'

'I don't know. Besides, there are a dozen more inquisitors currently on Terra who might equally be in the frame for the position. I said no to any kill-missions and I mean it.'

'So what do you propose to do about the situation?'

'That is for me to worry about. In Lansung's absence, thanks be to the Emperor for small mercies, it is possible for the Lord Commander to grant provisional first tier status to one of the other High Lords not in the Twelve. I have spoken with Udo, privately, and he is prepared to extend full senatorial rights to the Grand Master of the Officio Assassinorum. I need the Senatorum to convene before Veritus' conclave begins so that Udo can forward the proposal and I can second it. You'll need to be there too.'

'All very good, but I fail to see why you needed to tell me this with such urgency.'

'One of Veritus' companions has gone missing.'

'Machtannin? Yes, I know.' As soon as he said the words Vangorich regretted his glibness. Before he could qualify his statement, Wienand was on her feet, pointing at the Grand Master.

'Ah! So you've lost him as well!'

'Momentarily misplaced, perhaps,' confessed Vangorich, who didn't like being caught in such an awkward position.

'Find him,' snapped Wienand. 'You know he's able to mask his truc form, though to what extent we can only guess. Not like one of your Callidus Assassins, I'd wager, but certainly capable of mimicking anyone of the same basic physical structure. Veritus brought him here for a reason, to replace somebody, I'm sure of it.'

'Replace whom?'

'If I knew that I wouldn't be here asking you to hunt him down, would I?' Wienand flexed her fingers in agitation. 'I consider Machtannin's absence to be a paramount threat at this time. If you find him, try to take him alive.'

'If that is not possible?'

'Make it possible. Let's hope he isn't disguised as someone important.'

'Very well. I assume I will receive no official notification of this mission?'

'Your assumption is correct. I would certainly never condone the Officio Assassinorum being deployed against a fellow inquisitor, as I made clear at the start of this conversation.'

Vangorich smiled and sighed.

'I do so like it when we are being absolutely clear. It makes my duties all the more pleasant. I shall deal with this both-ersome shape-changer. Make sure you get me onto the Council of Terra again.'

'Naphor incense when you've located Machtannin?'

'As you say, Wienand. I look forward to a summons to the Senatorum Imperialis.'

'And I look forward to a smudge of blue smoke.'

THIRTEEN

Port Sanctus – Vesperilles System

The politicking was, for the moment at least, forgotten. The endless charade of seniority and command had given way to a higher, purer purpose. Not in all his life as a Naval officer had Rafal Kulik witnessed anything as grand as he did the day the fleet of the Segmentum Solar fought the orks at Port Sanctus.

The reality of the situation was relayed by cold schematics on the main bridge display, but Kulik had seen enough battle that he could picture what was happening with his mind's eye. The flickering runes on the massive screen were more than just blue and red symbols. Each was a starship of the Imperial Navy.

The smallest were the frigates, destroyers and other escorts, small clusters of sigils representing squadrons, three, four and five ships strong. Some were only a few hundred yards in length, just large enough to mount a warp engine, crew compartments and a lance turret or torpedo tube.

At the other end of the scale were the four battleships.

Like the *Colossus* each was a fortress teeming with a crew of thousands, several miles long and laden with enough weaponry to raze cities and lay waste to continents. *Colossus* was not suited to the main line of battle, hence the flagship's position with the other carrier assets at the heart of the fleet. Kulik's role, along with the cruisers *Majestic, Knightly Endeavour* and *Lasutia*, was to provide fighter and bomber support for the rest of the fleet. From this position, Admiral Price would also be able to monitor the progress of the battle and make adjustments to the plan as required.

The massive Ascension-class battleship *Honourable Destruction* was leading the port line under the command of Captain Tiagus, while the *Unfriendly Encounter* and *Bloodhawk*, two Retribution-class vessels, formed the point of the starboard flotilla.

Behind the behemoths came an assortment of grand cruisers and cruisers, arranged as per the orders of Admiral Price to deliver a spread of torpedoes, weapons battery fire, lance shots and some minimal launch capacity.

Their plasma engines leaving trails across the firmament, the two lines of ships forged through the void towards the glittering spread of the ork-held asteroid belt. There were tens of thousands of individual asteroids in the field, millions probably, scattered across thousands of cubic miles. Many were chunks of ice no larger than fists – but on the larger and more stable asteroids the orks had built fortresses equipped with missile batteries, energy weapons and strange warp-powered displacement cannons. Added to this were the so-called rock forts – large asteroids fitted with engines and shields, turning them into crude starships.

More conventional ork vessels were loitering within the cover of the debris field too – blunt, gun-heavy raiders and larger attack ships the equivalent in strength to cruisers. For the moment they were trying to hide, lying dormant until the lead elements of the fleet came into range. However, whatever advances the orks had made in their gravity and warp technology, their discipline and radiation shielding had not improved with them. Flares of energy and sensor bursts constantly betrayed the orks' positions to the more sophisticated scanning arrays of the *Colossus*. This information was relayed to the rest of the fleet as they continued to close with the enemy.

Thirty-seven ships of the line in total. Thirty-seven capital ships gathered in one place for a single purpose – to crush the ork outer defences. Along with the two dozen escort vessels that swarmed around them, these ships would have been enough to stir Kulik's heart and fire his resolve. The fact that they were only a third of the Imperial Navy forces in the system almost made him burst with pride and excitement.

Sweeping on an arc a few hundred thousand miles in-system of the rimward fleet was Lansung's immediate command – the expedition force of the Battlefleet Solar. There were no less than seven battleships among the eighteen capital ships in the taskforce: enough firepower to wipe out entire civilisations. Lansung's ships would interpose between the rimward flotilla and the hundred or more ork ships in close vicinity to the attack moon in orbit around the sixth world.

Further out towards the system edge, a hundred thousand

miles from the *Colossus*, Commodore Semmes was leading the remains of the Segmentum Solar coreward fleet. Under the tentative command of Acharya the fleet had lost nearly a third of its strength to repeated ork attacks, although it was still roughly equal to the rimward fleet in raw numbers. More damning had been the sapping of morale, Kulik was sure. He knew Raphael Semmes by reputation, and, although another of Lansung's favourites, the commodore certainly was regarded as bolder and more decisive than Acharya. At the moment his flagship, the Torrent-class battleship *Widow's Grief*, was leading the coreward fleet on a charge to unite with Price's command. The two fleets would intersect the asteroid field from opposite directions roughly fifty thousand miles apart. At that stage the coreward fleet would come about alongside the rimward fleet and together at last they would turn and rendezvous with Lansung in preparation for the next phase of the attack.

Such was the plan, at least. It was, on the face of it, a sensible strategy. The vagaries of warp travel meant that any fleet travelling as a mass would be scattered to some degree, and it was standard Navy protocol for fleets to rendezvous at a predetermined point in the target system. Acharya, for reasons neither Kulik nor Price had been able to fathom, had been so intent upon striking a blow against the orks as soon as he arrived, possibly to ensure Price gained no share of the glory, that he had not allowed for fleet consolidation and had jeopardised the entire endeavour. The dramatic but drastic measures now required were the consequence of that headstrong action.

The strategic display was orientated with the *Colossus* at

the centre, so that the two lines astern of the rimward flotilla stretched up and down the main screen, the clusters of
escorts at set intervals along their length. Kulik stood in his
usual spot, hands clasped behind his back. Price was just
to his right, arms crossed as he stared at the range counter on the display. When it reached the agreed limit, the
admiral spoke up.

'Captain Kulik, please signal the fleet to assume ascending line by echelon to starboard.'

'Aye aye, admiral.' Kulik turned and nodded to Shaffenbeck, who passed the order to the communications officers.
'Ascending line by echelon to starboard.'

The manoeuvre was basic but no less impressive because
of that. Over the next few minutes, starting with the rear-
most vessels, the two lines of capital ships started to drift
up and to starboard, while the front ships drifted down and
to port. This created two parallel diagonal lines, slightly
overlapping on one plane, but with the tail of the port line
several thousand miles above the front of the starboard line.
In this formation the prow weapons of every ship could be
brought to bear, and Price wasted no time taking advantage of this fact.

'Fleet to fire torpedoes, full spread, three salvos.'

The order repeated down the ranks and a few seconds
later the main display bathed the bridge with yellow light.
The screen was filled with the registers of nearly a hundred
plasma, atomic and cyclonic torpedoes surging towards the
orks. Kulik followed their progress, followed by the second
salvo, and then the third was on its way before the first wave
of torpedoes had hit.

'Main view, vid-capture ahead,' said the captain, grinning. He glanced at Price. 'I want to see this!'

The admiral smiled in return, a little pensively, but Kulik had no time to worry about what concerns might be burdening the thoughts of his superior. The torpedoes were almost on their target. The closest peeled open, launching dozens of plasma and nuclear warheads each.

There was no need for enhancement or magnification. One moment the screen showed the asteroid field dimly glittering in the light of the distant star. The next, blossoms of pale blue and white erupted from one side to the other, blotting out the stars. Detonation after detonation rippled across the void, here and there the darker oranges and reds of secondary explosions, or the whirling, spiralling electrical storms unleashed by cyclotronic expansions.

Then the second wave caught up with the first and the display was repeated in all of its glory, and by the time the third wave of torpedoes struck debris had formed glittering sprays of light that twinkled and spread across the whole display.

On a secondary screen dozens of enemy marker sigils winked out of existence. There were cheers from the assembled officers, who stood as one transfixed by the destruction.

'Beautiful,' muttered Kulik, eyes wide with awe.

'All speed ahead!' barked Price, who appeared unmoved by the whole experience. 'Carrier flotilla is to launch all wings and take up support positions. Form lines of attack by squadron and prepare to engage the enemy.'

Snapped out of his appreciative fugue, Kulik relayed the order automatically.

'Lieutenant Shaffenbeck, stand all air crews to readiness. Gun crews are to await the command. Main display to tactical.'

The view on the huge screen switched from the fading glow of the torpedo detonations to a tri-d representation of the asteroid field, with the two lines of the rimward fleet approaching from beneath. The pair of columns were breaking apart as the cruisers and battleships assumed squadron formations outlined by Price before the engagement had begun. Shorter-ranged ships moved to the fore of the attack.

'*Colossus* to primary carrier group,' Kulik announced. 'Form on our position and launch interceptor wings. Bomber wings to be held in reserve until targets have been designated.' The captain nodded to Shaffenbeck, who gave the order for the flight decks to launch their fighters.

The torpedoes had driven the orks from their hiding places like beaters setting game birds to flight on a hunt. The alien vessels broke this way and that from the asteroids, scattered by the devastating salvos. Most came directly for the Imperial fleet, whatever subtlety they might have possessed now lost through a combination of battle-excitement and fear.

The first ork ships headed directly for the *Honourable Destruction*, seizing on the closest enemy to hand. They could not have picked a less suitable target, as the Ascension-class ship opened fire with its long-range prow batteries, smashing the shields of the oncoming ork ships with blazes of shells and rockets. Lance turrets arrayed along the dorsal spine of the battleship opened fire as it slowly changed heading to starboard. Beams of pure energy sliced through the shieldless ork attack ships, turning one, then another and then a third into exploding clouds of fragments and gas.

Behind the dissipating remains of these vessels the remaining orks did their best to alter course away from the *Honourable Destruction*. Their manoeuvring was slow and clumsy, and by the time they had arranged themselves on new headings the *Bloodhawk* and the *Unfriendly Encounter* had parted from each other, creating a gap of several thousand miles between them for the enemy ships to pass through. The two battleships opened up with their full broadsides as the orks made a dash for the open stars between them. The void was filled with plasma bursts and the blur of immense projectiles. The first four ork ships, none of them larger than an Imperial destroyer, were utterly annihilated by the outpouring of fire. Two more were surrounded by the crackling auras of their overloaded shields while the rest hastily burned navigation thrusters in a fresh attempt to assume different courses.

By now the lead elements of the fleet were moving inside the dust and gas clouds that shrouded the edges of the asteroid field. Dragging his eyes away from the display, Kulik glanced at Price, who was standing bolt-straight, jaw clenched. Although he had voiced no concerns earlier, it was obvious that the admiral was unhappy about entering the asteroid field. He looked full of nervous energy, trembling slightly, fists clenching and unclenching by his sides as he held himself immobile against the urge to pace or speak.

A few rock forts and asteroid bases had survived the torpedo onslaught, but not enough to cause any real harm to the lead battleships. The three massive vessels were bathed in the purplish glow of their void shields as they ploughed through the swirling gases and dust. Missiles streaked past the ships from deeper within the field, launched by the ork bases.

Seven ork ships, three of them at least cruiser-sized, had broken past the battleships. Instead of heading into open space, the orks could not fight their warrior desires and the alien vessels were turning for a confrontation with the cruiser lines of the fleet. It was a fight they could not hope to win, but Kulik had seen suicidal bravery before and knew that the greenskins could inflict considerable damage before they were destroyed. It was important to remember that this was simply a linking of the two fleets; the greater battle was yet to come. Every ship damaged or lost now would be sorely missed in the fight against the attack moon.

'Should we move in to support, admiral?' said Kulik. 'Our bombers can deal with the smaller ork ships while the cruisers deal with the larger ones.'

'No,' said Price. 'All bomber wings remain on standby. We're going to need every attack craft we can field if we're going to take on that ork star base.'

'Understood, sir,' said Kulik. The captain rubbed his chin, an instinctual action he had developed long ago in preference to showing dissent to a superior. The distraction always helped him hold his tongue. In this case he thought it unwise to risk the larger ships in exchange for some bombers, but he was not going to argue with Price about it.

'Send word to blue, magenta and gold squadrons to intercept at first opportunity,' Price said, rocking back and forth on his heels. 'Red and black squadrons are to flank the battleships and scan for enemy ships and installations. None of the orks are to escape. The last thing we need are damned greenskins dogging our heels when we go in for the final attack.'

'Aye aye, sir,' said Shaffenbeck, gesturing for Saul to transmit the admiral's orders. The captain waited for any orders specific to his ship but none were forthcoming. 'And the *Colossus*, sir? What are we to do?'

The unspoken part of the question asked why a fully combat-capable battleship was being held back rather than committed to the attack. Price must have picked up on the captain's subtext.

'No fresh orders, captain,' the admiral said sharply, jaw clenched with irritation. 'The carrier group will remain on current station. I am not risking this ship and her launch capabilities just so that you don't feel left out, Rafal.'

'Aye aye, sir,' Kulik replied with a nod of salute. He turned an eye towards the screen where the rest of the fleet was surrounding the ork ships and pounding them to ruin with their guns.

Saul caught the captain's eye and subtly directed his superior to join him at the gunnery console a little further from the admiral. Catching Shaffenbeck's gaze, the lieutenant overseeing the targeting matrices suddenly realised that he had urgent business at the comms desk and moved to attend to that duty, leaving the two officers alone with the monitoring servitors.

'You seem agitated, sir,' said Shaffenbeck, keeping his voice low as the two of them stood side-by-side looking at the main display. 'A moment of pause and reflection might help you regain some equilibrium.'

'I don't know why Price is so reluctant to commit the flight wings,' said Kulik. 'He's had further communication from Lansung, no doubt outlining the Lord High Admiral's plan for the attack moon.'

'And why is that such a cause for concern?' Shaffenbeck indicated the tactical display with a flick of his head. 'The battle seems almost won.'

'Because if Price is under orders to keep the carriers at the back for this battle, it has to mean as sure as a Navigator's got a third eye we're going to be slap-bang right in the front of the next one.'

FOURTEEN

Phall – orbital

The battle-barge *Abhorrence* dwarfed the *Achilles* as the Space Marine vessel moved closer to receive a shuttle from the Naval patrol ship. Standing out further in orbit were a dozen other ships, of varying size and potency, from a number of different Chapters. Not all of the Successors had yet responded, but Koorland had weighed up the number that had arrived against the urgency of the situation and he had decided the time was right to hold council.

Marshal Bohemond of the Black Templars had agreed to have the *Abhorrence* act as host for the Chapter council, as not only was it the largest vessel in the system but Bohemond was the longest-serving Chapter commander present.

On the shuttle heading for the *Abhorrence* Koorland sat across from Lieutenant Greydove, who had insisted on accompanying the Space Marine to his destination for the sake of appearance. To his credit the young commander had obliged Koorland's demand to come to Phall without

complaint and once the *Achilles* had been set on course the
lieutenant had run a sharp, disciplined crew.

'What do you hope to achieve?' asked Greydove. The lieutenant leaned forward as far as the bars of his grip harness
would allow. 'Do you think the authorities will allow you
to get away with this? You've gone rogue, captain, is what
they'll say. They'll hunt you down.'

'Who will?' said Koorland. 'The High Lords? The Adeptus Terra? The Inquisition? They have far greater concerns
at the moment.'

'That may be, but I can see that you are not wholly comfortable with this.'

Koorland remained silent for a while. There was no reason to indulge the Naval officer's curiosity, and he owed no
explanation for any other reason. For all that, Greydove was
right. Koorland did have reservations, exceptionally grave
ones. He would not be able to share them with the Successors, not without causing offence or sowing doubt, but
they gnawed at his thoughts. The lieutenant made as good
a confidant as anybody.

'Bohemond,' said Koorland. 'Marshal of the Black
Templars.'

'What of him?'

'He has a reputation. More than that. The Black Templars
are a force apart. They claim lineage from Rogal Dorn as do
the rest of us, but they cleave to their own code and prac-
tices. I do not know if I can find common ground with him.
He is... headstrong.'

'Stubborn? Surely you can gain the support of others and
win him over.'

'If that is how it is, I will be well-pleased. However, I think that Bohemond may raise objections and I do not have authority to bargain with him.'

Greydove looked as though he was about to speak, but after a glance at the Space Marine he shook his head and remained silent.

'What is it?' demanded Koorland. 'What are you thinking?'

'You are the last of the Imperial Fists,' the lieutenant said, hesitantly. 'That makes you, by default, Chapter Master. You are Bohemond's equal.'

Koorland considered this. 'By default? That is no great claim to position.'

'I disagree. In your case, it is the greatest claim. The rest of the Chapter perished, but you survived. That makes you not remarkable but miraculous. Surely you have the blessing of the Emperor.'

'Superstitious nonsense,' grumbled Koorland, but the lieutenant did have a point behind the religious facade. 'There is something to what you say. However, will the others agree with your position, or simply see an upstart captain demanding action of his superiors?'

'That very much depends on you, captain,' Greydove said quietly. He looked at his hands clasped in his lap, his gaze flicking up occasionally to Koorland. 'You showed no lack of authority in taking my ship.'

'That was little challenge,' said Koorland. He saw the shame and hurt in Greydove's gaze and realised that he was misunderstood. 'Not because of you, but because of me. I am of the Adeptus Astartes. My size is intimidating, and the legends that surround my kind give me gravitas not even the greatest of Naval officers could match. I could be the least of my Chapter, yet even knowing nothing of me mortal men cannot help but defer to my will. If it is of any merit, you should know that you have my respect and, I believe, continue to have the respect of your crew.'

With a slightly abashed smile, Greydove met Koorland's gaze.

'It is of merit, thank you.' The smile faded and the lieutenant's brow furrowed. 'But why should you care? Forgive any impudence, but why would a captain of the Imperial Fists be concerned about the feelings of a lowly Naval lieutenant? Surely you have weightier matters to focus on?'

'Credit and honour to those who have earned it,' said Koorland. 'I make no exception in my remarks, for your conduct has been as worthy of praise as if you were a sergeant under my command who had shown similar qualities.'

The two of them fell silent, leaving Koorland to contemplate the exchange. A few minutes later the clank of the landing gear on decking announced their arrival aboard the *Abhorrence*. Greydove released his harness first and stood up. Koorland waited a few more seconds, gathering his thoughts.

'What is the worst that could happen?' said Greydove.

'The last of the Imperial Fists will be ridiculed for his pretensions of grandeur, so that the memory of my Chapter will end not only with extinction but infamy?'

'All right,' said Greydove, taken aback by Koorland's bleak forecast. 'And the best?'

'The Successors acknowledge that they must come together in the Imperium's hour of need and we are able to the destroy the Beast.' Koorland thought about what he said, comparing his goals with the price of failure. He pushed up his harness and faced Greydove, offering a hand in friendship with a smile. The lieutenant took it. 'You are right, of course. The rewards outweigh the risks, the cause justifies the action. Even if I am to be plunged into ignominy there is still every chance that my brothers in the other Chapters will be able to make common purpose. Thank you.'

'You may not believe it, but I think that the Emperor has chosen you for a greater purpose,' said Greydove. 'Of all the Imperial Fists, you have been spared. It is an honour to be the last, not a burden. I know nothing of Space Marines and their ways, nor of your Chapter, but in the small time since we met you have proven to be resourceful, determined, loyal and courageous. Everything the legends tell us to expect of the Adeptus Astartes. Your brothers, those that were left at Ardamantua, would be proud to have you represent them.'

Koorland smiled at these words, and yet what might be hollow, thoughtless praise struck a chord in the captain. He did not believe himself chosen by any higher power, but he was certain that he would carry himself according to the best traditions of his Chapter. He was an Imperial Fist – *the* Imperial Fist – and it was in his power to make that mean something.

The door hissed open and a ramp clanged down to the landing bay deck. A squad of Black Templars, their burnished ebon armour gleaming in the bay lights, waited with bolters at the salute. With them stood a warrior in more ornate armour, a red-crested helm under his left arm, a drawn power sword in his right hand. The officer stepped forwards as Koorland descended the ramp.

The Black Templar raised the hilt of his sword level with his chin, blade upright, in a mark of respect. Koorland placed a fist against the eagle on his chest in reply.

'I am Castellan Clermont. I am to convey you to the Marshal and Chapter Masters.' The castellan lowered his sword and carefully sheathed it before offering a hand in friendship. Koorland shook it gratefully.

'My thanks for the welcome, Clermont.' The two of them started walking across the massive bay, their escort falling in behind as the pair headed between the dormant Thunderhawk gunships. 'It makes me realise that I have been too long from the company of my fellow Space Marines.'

'You are amongst brothers again, Koorland. Harbour no doubts in that regard.'

It took a few minutes to reach the hall where the council was to be held. Clermont announced Koorland as two Black Templars swung open the great double doors, and then led the Imperial Fists captain within.

The hall was bedecked with trophies and banners, every square foot of wall covered with gilded skulls, tattered remnants of enemy standards and icons, pieces of tile, timber and masonry from conquered citadels. The floor was obsidian, as was the long table at which sat the council of Chapter Masters; the four of them turned questioning eyes on Koorland as he entered.

Bohemond was instantly recognisable, sat at the head of the table flanked by two banner bearers carrying the Chapter standard and a long pennant in the colours of the

Marshal's personal heraldry. Clermont advanced ahead of Koorland to join his commander and the group of Space Marines around him.

Koorland also recognised Issachar, whose pale armour was in total contrast to Bohemond's. The Chapter Master of the Excoriators was well known for his bionic arm, which was a plated mass of bare metal and cables; more precisely, known for the manner by which he had come to need it following an overly competitive honour duel with Marshal Bohemond during a previous disagreement. His artificial fingers tapped out a complex rhythm on the surface of the table, which stopped when his gaze met Koorland's.

The Chapter Master's false hand formed a fist that moved to his forehead, lips and chest in quick succession in a sign of fraternity. Koorland met the gesture with a simple nod.

Behind Issachar stood three warriors, one in the livery of the Chaplains and two that bore markings of the Librarium. The Black Templars occasionally threw menacing stares at the pair of psykers but the Excoriators feigned ignorance of their brothers' antipathy.

Opposite Issachar was a warrior that Koorland did not know. His armour bore no livery at all, the drab grey ceramite coloured only by heat swirls and splashes of dried blood. Only one Chapter that Koorland knew of did not paint their armour – the Fists Exemplar. The warrior was flanked by a Space Marine bearing the burnt remnants of a trapezoid banner and another with a long spear held in both hands.

Last at the table was Chapter Master Quesadra of the Crimson Fists. The Crimson Fists were almost as numerous as the Black Templars contingent, with two banner bearers, a cup-holder and three more Space Marines with thunder hammers held across their chests.

Their commander's armour was highly polished, shining in the light that spilled from the chandeliers above the table, shoulder pads inlaid with sapphire-like stones, the red circled fist of the Chapter icon picked out in delicately faceted rubies. Quesadra regarded Koorland in the same manner a warrior might size up a potential foe, mentally measuring his capabilities. To Koorland it felt as if those bright blue eyes were stripping him down to the soul, and he was relieved when Quesadra turned his laser-like gaze on Bohemond.

Faced with the grandeur and panoply of these mighty leaders Koorland felt inadequate in his plain, damaged battleplate. Doubts crowded his thoughts as he advanced across the tiles, the clang of his tread echoing around the large hall. Who was he to call upon these leaders and legends? Greydove was a normal man, easily impressed by those with superior physique and skill. The warriors that awaited Koorland at the table were of an order far above a lieutenant in the Navy.

Koorland realised that his actions were not those of a brave survivor, but those of a foolish, petulant child. How did he dare refuse the will of the High Lords? What did he hope to achieve here? It was petty of him to place his desires above the needs of the Imperium. The worst conceit was the notion that he could still make a difference, that somehow he could single-handedly save the reputation of the Imperial Fists. What arrogance, they would say.

Stopping beside the chair at the bottom of the table, directly opposite Bohemond, Koorland paused and took a deep breath. He looked at the officer from the Fists Exemplar.

'I am Koorland, of the Imperial Fists. I have the honour of knowing the names and titles of the others assembled here, but I regret that you have me at a loss.'

'Thane,' said the Space Marine. He hesitated before continuing, a flicker of a tic in his right eye. 'Chapter Master Thane, these last few weeks.'

'By my honour, I make acquaintance,' said Koorland, bowing before he seated himself.

'You are welcome, Captain Koorland,' said Bohemond, his voice booming across the hall. 'There is sense in us coming together to share intelligence of the foe and strategy for their destruction. We have spent some time appraising one another of our efforts, and I do not wish to waste time repeating such reports, but for the benefit of our new arrival I would make a quick summary of the situation.'

Bohemond looked around the table and there were no objections raised.

'Good,' he continued. 'The orks continue to press towards Terra on all fronts and the situation, already dire, is threatening almost total collapse. Almost. Having extracted our brothers in the Fists Exemplar from their fortress-monastery I have been calling together several crusades still operating in the Segmentum Solar. As you might expect, there is little to appeal to my marshals in these relatively calm systems and so the majority of our crusades are much further from the Imperial centre. It will take time for them to arrive.'

'Such calmness has occluded proper recognition of the threats at hand,' said Issachar.

Bohemond scowled, perceiving the comment to be an accusation, but he pressed on with his report without argument.

'It has fallen to us and the Crimson Fists in particular, as well as Chapters of other heritage, to wage the mobile war against the ork attackers. The Imperial Navy stands almost idle. We have filled the breach as best we can, but we have not the numbers to stand and fight at every contested star system. The orks move closer and closer to Terra each day while the Imperial Guard twiddle their thumbs on their mustering fields and the Imperial Navy watches with disinterest. If I could spare the bolts I would fall upon these traitors myself, but the orks are enough opposition for the moment. When the orks are driven back there will be time to punish those who have so easily forgotten their oaths.'

'Report arrives daily of another system fallen, another ork incursion, all accounted to the ravages of the Beast,' said Quesadra. 'We attack when we can, but we kill hundreds when we need to kill thousands, thousands when we must slay millions. We come to the aid of the Imperium as ancient oaths decree, but the Imperium seems unable to fight for itself. Not since Ullanor have we seen such a greenskin threat. Their numbers are beyond measure and matched by greater cunning than we have ever thought possible. Even as the orks are coordinated and focused, the forces of the Imperium are scattered and beset.'

'Let us not forget the sacrifice of many brave thousands that have given their blood defending their homes,' added Thane. 'They have taken a toll of the alien invaders also.'

A few of the Space Marines bowed their heads in silent thanks. Koorland did likewise, remembering his dead wall-brothers.

'Yes, but the sacrifices will not be swiftly concluded,' said Issachar. He glanced at Bohemond and received a nod of permission to continue. 'The issuing of the Last Wall protocol is a grave matter, but I think it is just this situation for which the Primarch intended it. The Imperium is beset by a foe that will likely triumph over other forces. No Chapter alone can stand against this menace and so the bonds of old, forged by the Emperor's hand and broken by the dictate of the Lord Commander, must be joined again. The sons of Dorn will stand united once more.'

'Indeed!' Bohemond's voice boomed across the hall. It dropped in volume as he continued with furrowed brow. 'I was surprised to find that it was not Cassus Mirhen that had sent the herald signal.'

'The Chapter Master is dead,' replied Koorland.

'A tragedy we have recently experienced,' said Thane, nodding in sympathy. 'He was a great leader. You are the surviving ranking captain, I assume?'

'The only survivor,' said Koorland quietly.

'And tell me, Captain Koorland, why it is that you come here alone, aboard an Imperial Navy vessel no less?' asked Bohemond, darting a look of annoyance at Thane's interruption. 'Where are your warriors and the rest of the fleet? You call us to the Last Wall and yet you come alone.'

'You misunderstand me, brothers.' Koorland bowed his head. 'I was not the only surviving officer at Ardamantua. I was the only survivor.'

Silence greeted this declaration.

Quesadra started to say something but the words died on his lips. Koorland looked at each of the Space Marines around the table and saw the same emotions in their expressions: hardened warriors brought to a standstill by confusion, anger, pity. It was the last that caused him the most pain and sent him surging to his feet.

'The Imperial Fists are no more,' he said, and speaking aloud the fact made the shame of it surge through Koorland. 'Save for me, they are all dead.'

He swallowed hard. He had faced death without fear a thousand times. He had been wounded, three times grievously, and now ripped back from the edge of oblivion by the ministrations of the tech-priests. Even during the horrors of Ardamantua Koorland had never felt scared, not truly. To stand here and say what he was about to say was the most terrifying experience of his life. He did not know what was going to happen as soon as he uttered the words. The future was a black abyss waiting to swallow him, but there was nothing else to be done but to plunge headlong into its dark embrace.

He looked at each of the Chapter Masters in turn and said the words that no son of Dorn wanted to hear. They were words that signified loss. More than that, a defeat so great, so shameful, that to anyone not of the Imperial Fists or Successors the words might seem trite. Yet to those who had Dorn's gene-seed it was a statement that would make such honoured blood run cold, an admittance of the worst failure imaginable.

'The final wall has fallen.'

FIFTEEN

Port Sanctus – inner system

'All hands! All hands! Prepare for fleet address! All hands! Attention for the Lord High Admiral!'

Shaffenbeck's voice boomed out over every internal comms system across the *Colossus*, and the order was being repeated across the dozens of ships heading in-system towards the ork attack moon. The greater part of the greenskins' strength still lay ahead, as scores of vessels rushed out from the star base's vicinity to confront the Imperial attack. The sensor team aboard the *Colossus* had calculated the enemy strength at roughly forty-eight capital-sized ships and over a hundred smaller vessels.

'Where did so many ships come from?' Kulik asked Price as the two of them sat in the communications cabin waiting for Lansung's speech. Neither of them were excited by the prospect of the Lord High Admiral's bombastic self-aggrandisement and so they had cloistered themselves away from the main bridge for the moment. 'I mean, not just here, but all across the segmentum? If every attack moon has a fleet this size, that's decades, centuries of building.'

'Yes, but not all of it by the orks.'

Price spread out pict-captures from the fleet of the ork vessels they had destroyed. Many were ghastly constructions, seemingly thrown together as much as they were designed. They sprouted improbably large and armoured gun turrets, packed weapons decks, oversized engines and outlandish decoration.

Quite a few, however, were recognisable as having once been other types of vessels. Kulik saw many Imperial ships, from destroyers up to heavy cruisers, that had been somehow taken by the orks and retro-fitted in their own fashion. Even just amongst those already encountered, there were enough captured Navy vessels to form a sizeable flotilla. There were also dozens of merchant ships that had been up-gunned and up-armoured with the simple addition of weapons turrets and shield generators.

'That explains it in part, but they've got more of our ships than the Battlefleet Solar. How have they not been noticed missing?'

'It seems the orks have been... stockpiling for some time.'

'Stockpiling? You mean that the orks have been deliberately building their forces somewhere, waiting for this moment to attack?'

'I don't know about waiting for this moment, but the massed fleets, the attack moons, all have arrived almost simultaneously,' Price said with a heavy sigh. 'It's impossible to put this down to coincidence. There is a far grander purpose behind these attacks, I'm sure of it. As to where and how the orks managed to build these things, that's a mystery for another day. There're huge tracts of space that have never been surveyed, even with our current Naval strength. It only takes a few systems to slip past us to hide a fleet this size.'

'But... *orks* doing this?' Kulik simply could not get his head around the idea. 'Orks laying low and strategising in this manner is unheard of. It is, to put it a certain way, totally alien to them. I know we hardly know anything about them really, there's been few encounters over the last centuries, but they've always been aggressive, invasive.'

'Something has changed, that's for sure,' said Price. He gathered up the vid-captures into a pile and stacked them neatly to one side. 'These damned orks not only have a plan, they have a larger objective, something we're not seeing.'

'Other than a steady encroachment, there's been no pattern to their attacks,' said Kulik. 'They don't seem to be heading anywhere in particular. Some have been strategically important systems, some are backwaters that nobody had heard of until they were invaded. If they've been hoarding ships all of this time, centuries probably, surely it would be for something more specific than just a huge jolly war?'

'I don't just mean the orks overall, I mean the orks here, in Port Sanctus. This fleet is large in comparison to some of the scattered reports we received. There must be something about the dockyards that they really want, pulling in a whole damned armada to get it. Why did Acharya have to choose this system of all the ones the orks have attacked to prove himself?'

'It's self-sustaining, isn't it? The orks must have known about the shipyards, and if they can take them they know they can build even more ships.' Kulik glanced at the chronometer. Lansung's speech would be received shortly.

'If that's true, then perhaps it is best that we're here. There's no telling how much stronger they'll get if they keep taking facilities and systems at this rate. Every conquest seems to be fuelling more, but to what end?'

'I think you're giving them too much credit, sir,' said Kulik, standing up. 'I doubt they even know why they're doing half of this. Maybe there is a smart ork out there, something more intelligent than we've met before, but it certainly isn't in control. It's a figurehead, something like that. There's not an ork in the universe that could prepare and coordinate an invasion like this.'

'I hope you're wrong,' said Price, following Kulik as the captain made his way back to the bridge in anticipation of the Lord High Admiral's address.

'How so, sir? Do you really think it would bode well for the Imperium if there was such a creature?'

'It would be worse for us if there isn't. If the Beast really is behind this calamity, someone can find it and kill it and bring this invasion to an end. If not... I have no idea what we can do to stop them.'

With this sobering thought in mind Kulik stepped back onto the bridge just in time for Saul's announcement.

'Incoming live-feed transmission. Fleet-wide address from the *Autocephalax Eternal*, flagship of Lord High Admiral Lansung.'

'Open channels for reception, broadcast to all stations,'

Kulik said as he took his place at his usual spot at the centre of the bridge.

'All hands! All hands! Prepare for fleet address! All hands! Attention for the Lord High Admiral!'

On the big screen Lansung's face appeared, as round and massive as an ork attack moon. Fortunately for most of the crew they would be receiving audio only and did not have to watch a sweat bead almost as big as Kulik's fist sliding down the cheek of the Lord High Admiral and into the fold between two of his chins.

'We are about to embark on a mission that is vital to the continued future of the Imperium,' announced Lansung. 'What happens over the next few hours could well determine the course of mankind's dominance amongst the stars for the next hundred generations. I know you do not wish to spend these next few minutes listening to me babble on about glory, honour and respect. You have all been raised in the finest traditions of the Navy and I have only a short message, which I am sure you will all understand and take to heart.'

Lansung drew in a deep breath and Kulik thought he saw uncertainty in the plate-sized eyes staring down at them. The Lord High Admiral closed his eyes, perhaps in contemplation, or perhaps in resignation, it was impossible to tell. He spoke without opening them.

'The Emperor expects every man to do his duty.'

As the last word echoed around the bridge the transmission ended. Kulik wondered what could possibly lead a man like Lansung, a man who had demonstrated on every previous occasion a need to hear his own voice at tremendous length, to deliver such a short oration.

'He's scared,' whispered Price, as if guessing Kulik's thoughts. 'He really isn't sure if we're going to win today.'

'I'll settle for surviving,' said the captain. 'That'll do me just fine.'

'I don't think that's an option, Rafal,' said the admiral. 'If we don't destroy those orks, none of us is getting out of Port Sanctus alive.'

Comforting, thought Kulik. Just the sort of encouragement I've been hoping for.

The captain scratched his chin for a few seconds.

'Aye aye, sir,' he growled.

SIXTEEN

Terra – the Imperial Palace

The moment the door swished open Wienand knew something was wrong.

For a start, an amber light glowed dimly on the entry access panel on the wall to her left. Somebody with inquisitorial clearance had entered her official chambers, other than herself or Rendenstein. In itself this was no cause for unduc alarm, but it was unusual for anybody to come here when Wienand was not present.

The second factor that made Wienand stop just inside the door was the silence. Rendenstein was supposed to be here, and that always meant the faint buzz of a digi-reader or the clatter of a terminal keypad, even just the soft tread of Rendenstein as she made her random security checks. There was nothing. The buzzing of the air circulation units had fallen silent. It was part of the defence features of the chambers that all electrical systems would cut out if an energy spike was detected. In this case it was probably a lasweapon discharge, although it could be something as simple as a power cylinder from a plasma weapon or even the field source for a power sword or other energy weapon. Even the crack of a bullet was enough to set off the delicate sonic detectors secreted throughout the offices.

Also, just beneath the keypad of the door security system was the faintest red smudge of a fingerprint. Wienand had instantly recognised it as blood. There was no trace on the keypad itself – wiped clean by the interloper, no doubt – but instinct told her that the blood belonged to Rendenstein.

Lastly, the real clincher was the door ahead of her at the end of the entryway. It was ajar, kept open by a heavy-soled boot. There was more blood on the tread. It certainly wasn't the sort of footwear Rendenstein would have been wearing.

Paused with the door still open behind her, one hand half-stretched towards the security pad, Wienand considered her options.

She had been summoned here by Veritus. The conclave was due to begin in an hour, in the Octagon. Obviously someone had decided to pre-empt the proceedings, or otherwise interfere.

In Wienand's estimation that person was most likely Veritus himself. Maybe Najurita had been more reluctant to participate than the old inquisitor had originally hoped, or perhaps Veritus simply preferred to settle matters the way they had been settled in the old days.

Another option was that she had been betrayed by Vangorich, perhaps in trade for the support of Veritus. She dismissed the possibility. If Vangorich really wanted Wienand dead she wouldn't be alive to think about it. The Officio Assassinorum did not give second chances, not here on Terra where everything was to their advantage.

It was not safe to stay here.

Wienand turned around and strode back into the corridor, left hand towards the sensor pad by the door, her seal ring pulse-transmitting a signal to close the portal. She whispered a three-part code to initiate full lockdown and then turned right, heading towards the monorail terminal a few hundred feet further into the Imperial Palace.

The station was empty, as Wienand expected. The mono-shuttle was for Inquisitorial personnel only – and Vangorich, apparently, Wienand remembered with irritation – and was the only way to access the inner chambers of the Inquisitorial enclave. One shuttle was at the platform, on the westbound track leading to the main part of the Palace via the Adeptus Ministorum Senatorum chapels. The eastbound track, which would take her to the main transport hub at the Eternity Terminus, was devoid of carriages.

There were two ways to read this discovery. The first was to assume that whoever had breached the inner chambers had then exited towards the transport hub. The second, more paranoid and likely version of events, was that someone had anticipated Wienand's attempt to flee and was manoeuvring her towards the Ministorum enclave for a particular reason.

It also made sense that she was cut off from the transport hub; from there she could requisition an ornithopter to take her directly to the main Inquisitorial Fortress under the south polar ice cap. Her allies were there, as were six companies of Inquisitorial storm troopers and no doubt a few other mercenary types currently in the employ of one inquisitor or another who would be more than willing to engage in hostilities.

She suddenly realised how isolated she was here, and

remembered the words of Veritus. He had said that she had become too close to the Senatorum, and perhaps he meant geographically as well as metaphorically. By holding her offices here, in the Senatorum palaces rather than at the polar bastion, she was cut off from the Inquisition.

Thinking she heard a distant footfall behind her echoing down the passage, Wienand darted a look down the colonnaded corridor towards her chambers. She saw nothing, but was now convinced that someone was there, perhaps out of sight, perhaps cloaked somehow. Her enemies – it had to be Veritus – had access to all kinds of archeotech if needed.

She jumped into the open-topped mono-shuttle, closed the gate behind her and sat down on one of the benches. The shuttle was about five yards long, barge-like in shape, with four benches running its width like the thwarts of a rowing boat. Though it had a metal infrastructure, the exterior of the shuttle was covered in ornately carved wood and panelling lacquered a deep red, with polished brass fittings. Rows of terminal panels were fixed in front of each bench. Detecting her presence, the carriage's machine-spirit sprang into life, illuminating a map display on a board in front of Wienand. She tapped in her cipher key and then selected the Cathedral of the Saviour Emperor as her destination.

There was safety in public, she reasoned. The Cathedral was one of the greatest sites for pilgrims all across the galaxy to visit and at any time there were tens of thousands of them living and waiting in the Piety Dorms that stretched for several miles around the shrine. It was easy to get lost there, and Wienand needed to get lost very urgently.

The shuttle rattled into life as gear teeth bit into the rack running the length of the track, lurching the carriage forwards. The clanking increased in speed as the motor accelerated to full capacity, yellow lamps springing into life ahead and behind as the shuttle passed into the tunnel mouth at the end of the platform.

Leaning forward, Wienand reached under the bench and used her ring-transmitter to open the auto-bolt on the reinforced locker beneath. She pulled open the front to reveal several guns and pistols. She selected a lightweight bolt pistol and loaded it, placing it in the pocket of her coat. As added protection she pulled out a snub-nosed laspistol and tucked that inside her boot. Moving to the locker to her right she repeated the action and retrieved several blind and concussion grenades. Another locker yielded up a shock maul that slipped nicely up her sleeve and a sheathed vibroknife that she tied to her waistband.

As the shuttle clattered along in the gloom of its own lamps, Wienand took stock once more. Rendenstein was still alive, she was sure of it, if only because her bodyguard and assistant was fitted with an internal pulse monitor that had not activated. She might be captured or hurt, but Rendenstein's heart was still beating.

It was impossible to hear anything over the clattering of the rack-and-pinion engine of the carriage, but Wienand could not shake the feeling that someone was following along the track behind her. She twisted on the bench and glared back. There was nothing in the twin cones of yellow projected by the rear lamps. In the darkness beyond, who could say?

In the fourteen tortuous minutes it took for the shuttle to clank and wheeze its way to the Cathedral of the Saviour Emperor, Wienand formulated a plan.

It was a very simple plan. She would lose herself amongst the human crush of the Piety Dorms. That was as far as it went. Survival was her only goal in the foreseeable future. Once that was assured Wienand could expend thought and energy on something loftier, like finding out who was trying to kill her and how she was going to respond.

The implications of what Veritus had done horrified Wienand but she forced herself to think through the consequences. The Inquisition was meant to be a free-form, self-regulating organisation. In fact, the term organisation was misleading. The Inquisition was officially recognised by the Senatorum Imperialis and the rest of the Imperium, but other than that it had no formally mandated structure, duties or remit.

In essence there was no Inquisition as such, just inquisitors. Each inquisitor, a bearer of the Emperor's Seal, was a power unto himself or herself. Nobody was quite sure who had appointed the first inquisitors – or even if anyone had appointed them and they had not simply assumed the role for themselves. Over a thousand years later, it was still true that an inquisitor was the only authority that could bestow the Emperor's Seal to another. Not the High Lords, the entirety of the Adeptus Terra nor the Mechanicus could grant such power to one man or woman.

Necessity had required a certain amount of support and infrastructure, and ad-hoc solutions had, over the centuries, gathered gravitas and traction to become quasi-formal institutions. The Inquisition as an entity had grown, as had the role of Inquisitorial Representative. Wienand had read some of the earliest Senatorum reports and it seemed that in those early decades the Inquisitorial Representative had simply been whoever was on Terra and available at the time. That was when the Inquisition had been looking outward far more than inward; resurgent alien threats, the risk of the rise of forces allied to the Ruinous Powers.

It pained Wienand to consider the notion that perhaps Veritus had been right on some level. Maybe the Inquisition had been tainted by association. The free-thinking, dynamic band of trusted investigators and agitators, judges and executioners, proselytisers and protectors had become something far greater, yet also diminished. The Inquisition possessed resources far beyond what it could have claimed even a century earlier, in terms of manpower, wargear and materiel. It had ships and soldiers, fortresses and libraries, communications nets, security protocols, sleeper cells, kill teams, relay posts, research stations and an untold number of agents, operatives, spies, infiltrators, slaved-servitors, pilots...

'Damn,' Wienand said out loud. 'That bastard Veritus is right.'

The whole point of the Emperor's Seal, the authority it represented, was to set the entire resources of the Imperium at the disposal of an inquisitor. If he or she needed an army, the Imperial Guard was required to oblige. If an inquisitor needed a ship, the Navy would provide. If someone was meant to be killed, there was the Officio Assassinorum. With a galaxy-spanning empire to draw upon, albeit fractured and impossible to govern, why did the Inquisition need these things for itself?

The answer was simple. The Imperium was broken. The offices and organisations meant to rule and control the vast interstellar swathes of mankind were simply unfit for the purpose. In fact, no institution would ever fit; the size of the Imperium and its scattered worlds prevented anything like meaningful communication and governance.

'Damn,' Wienand said again, as she realised the full extent of what Veritus intended. 'He means to use the Senatorum as the Inquisition's puppet. He thinks the Inquisition should control the Imperium.'

A hiss of hydraulics and a gentle squeak of brakes brought Wienand sharply back to the present. Veritus had to be stopped, but in due course. Wienand reminded herself of concern number one: survival.

The Inquisitorial shuttle bay was a concealed adjunct to a much larger transport station situated a few miles from the Cathedral of the Saviour Emperor. Glow-globes broke into dim life as the carriage coasted to a stop alongside a bare metal gantry of a platform. The carriage motors whined down to a low drone and then fell dormant. Wienand activated the nav-system once more, bringing the shuttle back to full life. She punched in the codes for dock three of the Widdershins Tower, location of the Cerebrium.

As the shuttle shunted forwards, Wienand jumped clear to the gantry and watched the carriage rattle on up the track. She wasted no time, darting up a set of metal steps at the end of the platform two at a time. She keyed in the combination of the lock-cycle barring the door at the top and slipped out onto the main concourse of Saviour Station.

The drone of hundreds of people greeted her and for the first time since setting foot in her chambers, Wienand allowed herself to hope that she might actually live through the next hour.

SEVENTEEN

Port Sanctus – Vesperilles System

A constant rumble shook the deck as the *Colossus'* guns kept up a rolling salvo of fire. The battleship's lances spat white beams at the ork ships swarming along the line of Imperial Navy vessels. Void shield generator overload warnings thrummed as return fire ploughed into the battleships and cruisers of the Emperor's Navy.

The greenskins had boiled out of the inner system like hornets streaming from a nest, dozens of smaller attack ships and a score of larger vessels that came hurtling directly for the fleet. Kulik had first taken the headlong charge as further proof that the orks were not as sophisticated as Price feared; such rush attacks had been the hallmark of many an ork raiding force for centuries. Lansung had ordered the fleet to split into lines of attack in response, hoping to break through the orks in a repeat of the attack on the asteroid field.

That was when the orks had revealed their first surprise. Rather than continue on their course directly towards the nearest ships, the alien warships had slowed and gathered their strength, turning their fury upon just two of the forming battle lines. The *Colossus* had been one of several ships that had borne the brunt of that first attack.

The *Seraphic Guardian, Terrible, Last Endeavour, Magnificent Fate* and *Klaus Magnate* had all surged forward in response to the call from Admiral Price to protect the flagship, but now the cruisers were embroiled in a messy fight with the smaller ork ships while the larger enemy vessels had broken away to concentrate their attack on the second line of Imperial ships.

Price was stalking back and forth across the bridge, grunting and muttering to himself. It was obvious that he had over-reacted to the first ork attack but it was too late to salvage anything meaningful from the situation.

'Damage crews to prioritise the energy grid and flight decks,' Kulik announced, adjusting his balance as another shockwave pulsed along the battleship. He glanced up at the screen showing the void shield generators and hull integrity data. More hits aft. The orks were very deliberately targeting the main engines. Shaffenbeck had evidently noticed the same thing.

'Do you think they're trying to cripple us before moving in for the kill, sir?' said the first lieutenant.

'Maybe,' replied Kulik, though he preferred a different explanation, which he voiced, just loud enough to make sure Price could hear it too. 'It might also be that they are trying to damage our engines to stop us getting anywhere near the attack moon. It might not be as impregnable as we feared.'

'One disaster at a time, captain,' Price said sharply. 'The

attack moon will wait for us to throw ourselves at it, no need to hurry the matter.'

Surprised, Kulik said nothing in response to the admiral's defeatist remark, but caught a look from Shaffenbeck out of the corner of his eye.

'Helm, bring us seven points to starboard and have every other fourth and sixth deck gun crew moved to their starboard batteries. I want a constant fire once we turn.'

Kulik studied the schematic a little longer. The cruisers had broken into pairs and were snaking their way to port, driving off the ork attack ships but leaving themselves vulnerable to several larger ork vessels moving up in a second wave.

'Have *Remarkable* and *Justified Annihilation* come about on the port side,' the captain told the comms officer. 'They are to cross our turn and assist the forward cruisers.' ·

Price stopped his pacing and looked at Kulik with narrowed eyes. *Remarkable* and *Justified Annihilation* were two Lunar-class ships, the newest in the rimward patrol flotilla. Although part of the rimward fleet they were also under the command of Kulik as commodore, and he was technically within his rights to issue orders. The admiral looked at Kulik for several long seconds, perhaps trying to work out if the captain was being insubordinate, before he shook his head and resumed his stalking.

A secondary detonation somewhere amidships caused the *Colossus* to shudder from prow to aft, the sudden movement almost throwing Kulik to the deck. Price stumbled, to be caught by an alert lieutenant who had been turning to report.

'Sir, we're detecting a strange energy surge from the ork ships to starboard.' Price pushed himself away from the officer and straightened his coat. Muttering some more, he turned and glared at the damage display on the main screen.

'Be more specific, lieutenant,' replied Kulik. 'What sort of energy surge? That ship looks too small to be warp capable.'

'It's like a small-scale transition, captain. I've never se–'

'Watch lieutenants on decks four and five report enemy boarding parties, sir!'

Price, Kulik and Shaffenbeck all turned as one towards the comms lieutenant who had issued the warning, then as one they all returned their attention back to the main screen. The nearest ork ship was at least three thousand miles away.

'Confirm that report, Mister Hartnell!' barked Shaffenbeck, striding towards the comms panel.

'More ork attackers, sirs!' the distraught lieutenant repeated. 'Decks fourteen and fifteen.'

'Teleport attack?' Price was incredulous. 'Those ships are far too small.'

'Confirm some form of warp portal excavation, captain,' said the officer at the sensor console. 'All three enemy ships have some kind of teleporter lock.'

'Where?' demanded Kulik.

The officer changed the main display and a series of green crosshairs sprang up on a rotating isometric display of the *Colossus*. There were breaches in seven different places. Blue icons represented the responding armsmen teams, closing in on the ork teleport attack sites from above and below.

'Emperor's blood, that's two decks below us!' Price took a few paces towards the comms officer. 'Tell the armsmen to prioritise the second boarding. They must protect the bridge!'

'Belay that order!' Kulik's command stopped Price in his

tracks. The admiral was enraged as he rounded on the captain, but Kulik cut off his superior. 'The first attack is right on top of the flight decks. We need to keep the launch bays operational. Officer of the watch!'

'Sir?' asked Shaffenbeck, stepping up.

'Admiral Price will have ship command, in my absence,' Kulik told him. The captain purposefully pulled free his service pistol and heavy sword. 'These are not just for parades.'

'This is highly improper, captain,' protested Shaffenbeck.

'Go with him, lieutenant,' said Price, mollified by Kulik's explanation. 'See that your captain does not get into too much trouble.'

Caught between his sense of duty and two conflicting orders, Shaffenbeck stepped first one way and then the other, gaze flicking between his superiors. Kulik shot him a meaningful glance and the lieutenant seemed to break his stasis and followed his captain towards the doors.

'Mister Hartnell,' Shaffenbeck addressed the lieutenant at the comms station, 'have Sergeant Latheram meet the captain at the top of the command deck third for'ard stairwell, with as many men from the upper companies as he can muster.'

'Have him arm defence squads from the lance crews, they'll be put to better use against the boarders than trying to hit fast attack ships,' added Kulik as the doors rumbled open just in front of him. He paused at the threshold and turned on his heel to look at Admiral Price. 'Leaving the bridge, with your permission, sir?'

'Aye, captain, carry on!' Price replied with a wave of the hand.

Outside the armoured confines of the bridge Kulik could immediately hear sounds of fighting echoing along the corridor. Shouts and small-arms fire rang from the metal walls. He broke into a gentle run with Shaffenbeck at his heel, heading for the closest stairwell down to the deck below.

'Mister Cabriot,' he barked, lifting his cuff-piece communicator to his mouth, 'with the admiral's assent, have helm move us away from the attack ships, and order all weapons batteries to target them as soon as they come to bear. Let's cut off the flow of reinforcements if we can.'

'Aye aye, sir,' came the crackling reply.

It took less than a minute to reach the top of the stairs but there was no sign of Sergeant Latheram and his armsmen. Kulik made towards the steps but Shaffenbeck grabbed his elbow and stopped him.

'We need to wait for the armsmen, sir,' said the lieutenant.

'That could be another five minutes, we've got men fighting and dying right beneath our feet, man!'

'All the same, sir, we can't do anything for them yet, unless we want to join them in the Emperor's locker box.'

'This isn't like you, Saul,' said Kulik, pulling free his arm. 'Never seen you back down from a fight, not in all the years we've served together.'

'It's the admiral, sir.' Shaffenbeck looked away, ashamed.

Kulik knew the mannerism well; the lieutenant wanted to say something but considered it too far outside his remit to utter the thoughts.

'Out with it, you know you can trust me, Saul. What about the admiral?'

'I don't trust him, not with the *Colossus*. He's been acting odd ever since Lord High Admiral Lansung arrived. No, before then. This feud with Acharya, that's what started it off.'

'Price is a decorated and capable commander, lieutenant,' Kulik said sternly. He saw a sudden fear in Shaffenbeck's eyes. Not the fear of the physical but fear of reprimand, of failing in honour or duty. It softened the captain's mood immediately. 'There's a lot at stake, you heard what Lansung told him. Price is under a lot of pressure.'

'I think he's buckling...' Shaffenbeck let the thought drift away as boots clattered on the stairs above them, heralding the arrival of Sergeant Latheram and his armsmen.

'Reporting as ordered, captain.' The gaunt warrant officer snapped off a salute. 'Got fifty men from the lance crews, sir, with shotters and boarding gaffes. Shall I lead the way, captain?'

Kulik could hardly refuse as the wiry man almost pushed his way past and shouted to his men to follow.

The armsmen of the *Colossus* wore the same deep blue as the officers, with red stripes on the legs and piping of the same on their plasteel-mesh-reinforced jackets. Their wore full-visored helms and rebreathers, and carried stubby shotguns and lascarbines – short-ranged but effective weapons perfect for the brutal and bloody work of shipboard combat.

Kulik started down the steps not far behind Latheram, with Shaffenbeck right behind him. The sergeant turned left at the bottom of the steps, heading aft, where the sounds of fighting were louder.

'Captain, we have two more teleport registers close to your position. One astern of c-section, one in the prow sensor access tunnels,' reported Lieutenant Cabriot.

'Sergeant, we need to head for'ard. There's another lot of greenskins attacking the sensor arrays. If they take them offline we'll be blind and deaf.'

'Right you are, sir,' said the sergeant. He performed an abrupt about-face, power maul on his shoulder, pistol in his other hand. 'This way, lads. Don't dawdle!'

Flashes of gunfire shone from the bare bulkheads a couple of hundred feet ahead of the party – the watch lieutenants on each deck were issued with keys to the firearms lockers when a ship went to general quarters. There were sporadic snaps of laser fire, but far more bass cracks and bangs from the orks' slug-throwers. Bestial growls and roars, punctuated by the wet slosh of blood, the snap of shattering bones and howls of pain, made Kulik glad he had listened to Saul and not dashed headlong into the melee.

In the light of the gunfight large, brutish shadows were thrown against the walls ahead. Kulik counted at least a dozen bodies strewn along the passageway before them, contorted and battered so badly they were barely recognisable as human. With a sinking heart the captain counted no orkish casualties amongst the dead.

'Captain, the tech-priests have locked down the sensor chambers and secured the prow bulkheads, but they say that the orks have brought cutting gear with them. They'll be through in a matter of minutes.' Hartnell sounded calm enough over the comm, but Kulik could imagine the tension on the bridge. Fighting a battle was bad enough, but doing so while hulking alien brutes were rampaging through your ship – and capable of teleporting an attack seemingly at will – was probably testing the nerves of even the bravest officers.

'Do you think they know what's in there, sir?' asked Shaffenbeck, looking paler than usual.

'I hope not,' said the captain. 'Because if this is a deliberate attack to cripple our sensors, the orks know a whole lot more about our ships than I'm happy about.'

'Best we stop them, eh, sir?' suggested Shaffenbeck with a forced smile.

'At the double, please, sergeant.' Kulik tried to exude confidence with his voice but his words sounded slightly shrill. 'Let's kill these orks before they cut through into the sensorium.'

As the company broke into a run, Kulik and Shaffenbeck surrounded by armsmen and shotgun-wielding ratings, the captain's hands started sweating profusely. It was odd, considering how dry his mouth had become.

They rounded a corner into the corridor leading to the first bank of scanners. Fortunately, for all their guile in targeting the ship's engines and trying to disable the scanning array, the orks were not so advanced that they had thought of leaving a rearguard. In fact, only about two dozen of them had stayed with the spark-spitting cutters at the bulkhead outside the sensor chambers. Presumably the others, having safely delivered the cutting crew to their objective, were off looking for more butchery and fun. Kulik would have breathed a sigh of relief had he not been out of breath from the running; commanding a capital ship was not always the most physically taxing of jobs and though he had made efforts to stay in shape, age was catching up with him. A glance at Shaffenbeck showed that the first lieutenant was at least reddening in the face a little.

One of the orks glanced back at the sound of tramping boots and let out a noise somewhere between a cry of alarm and a whoop of joy. Responding, the other greenskins turned as the first armsmen opened fire with their lascarbines, filling the passage with red bolts of light and the scent of ionising air. A few orks fell casualty to the salvo, but a plethora of pistols and stubby-nosed automatic weapons rose like a thicket around the survivors. Kulik slowed his run as he stared into the multitude of gun barrels.

The clatter of the orks' return fire combined with the boom of shotguns, deafening Kulik in the enclosed space. The captain fired his pistol into the face of an ork about forty feet in front of him. The las-blast ricocheted off the side of its head, leaving a scorch mark in its green flesh but doing no greater damage. Bullets screamed and whirred past Kulik – inches away, it felt.

Saul was yelling encouragement, urging on the ratings as more and more of them fell to the scything ork bullets.

'Up and at them, men of *Colossus*!' roared Kulik without really understanding what he was doing.

An armsman just in front of the captain fell sideways, his head and helmet scattering bloodily across the corridor. Two orks wielding the ramshackle cutting devices turned their equipment on the charging humans. Lightning arced, catching Sergeant Latheram and three more men in a tempest of black and green energy.

An unthinking rage fuelled Kulik as he thumbed the power switch of his sword. A flickering energy field flowed along the blade, casting bizarre, jolting shadows on the walls. A tiny, more rational part of the captain's mind screamed in terror, but it erupted from his mouth as a wordless bellow of defiance.

Around their captain, long boarding pikes held level, the lance gunners charged too, driving the tips of their gaffes towards the greenskins. Shaffenbeck had his sword in hand, its blade the near-transparent blue of tempered plasteel alloyed with ardamite crystal threads.

One-on-one the men of the battleship would have been no match for the bestial greenskins, but as a mass they pressed in, following their officers, united in purpose and momentum. Years spent working the aiming gears and exchanging the energy cells of the immense lance cannons had made the ratings tough, muscled men, and with the force of desperation and the shout of their lord and master ringing in their ears, they drove home their spears with irresistible force.

The orks crashed heavy mauls and cleavers against the metal-sheathed hafts of the boarding pikes, but to little avail. Pinioned in many places, the closest orks were pushed back into their companions, the men behind the pikes twisting the shafts as they had been taught, to drive their weapons even deeper through flesh.

Kulik stabbed the tip of his sword into the eye of a transfixed alien, ramming half the blade into its head to be sure. On his right, Shaffenbeck slashed the guts out of another greenskin. There was no room for parry and thrust, cut and riposte. The captain lashed out almost blindly; it was impossible to miss, his only care to avoid his crewmen with his wide swings. It was not so much swordsmanship as it was butchery skill.

Miraculously, Sergeant Latheram had somehow survived the strike from the electro-cutters, though his chest, left arm and half his face were a mass of burns. There was smoke drifting from his hair and the ragged remains of his clothes. A single eye stared wildly from the mass of scorched tissue, filled with such loathing that it scared Kulik. The sergeant brought his glowing power maul down onto the skull of an ork, crushing it with a single blow. Another sweep caved in the chest of another.

Kulik felt the armsmen surge again around him and was happy to be pushed back away from the melee for a moment, lashing out one last strike across the throat of an ork that was trying to bite the head from one of the pikemen. Shotguns barked, lethal even to the orks at this close range, shredding bodies and obliterating heads and limbs.

Kulik stumbled out of the side of the fighting, coming up hard against the bulkhead, almost collapsing as his head crashed against a stanchion. As ever, Shaffenbeck was just a step behind, in time to grab his captain to stop him falling over.

Wincing, stars dancing across his vision, Kulik turned his back to the bulkhead and eased himself against it, taking gasps of warm, sweaty air. The corridor was filled with battle-din – noises more animal than human or ork, shouts and sounds of flesh being ruined as the last of the aliens fought ferociously against the inevitable. Glancing around, Kulik could see at least a score of his own men dead, piled on the decking where they had been shot, cut down or clubbed to death.

It then fell eerily quiet, the only sound ragged panting

and the groans of the wounded ratings and armsmen. There was the bark of a shot. Men with shotguns and boarding pikes moved amongst the ork fallen, cutting and shooting off their heads to ensure they were dead. Kulik could see a few of the survivors tending to the casualties; an armsman whose arm had been ripped off was helped away as he numbly searched amongst the blood and gore for the missing limb.

'That's the last of them, sir!' Shaffenbeck said with a weary grin.

'No it isn't,' the captain replied, heaving in another breath. 'A whole bunch have split off and the Emperor alone knows where they've got to.'

A huge shudder along the hull almost knocked Kulik's head back against the bulkhead, reminding him that defeating the orks aboard was only one of his concerns. They were still in the midst of a massive space battle. He needed to get back to the bridge – Shaffenbeck was right that Price was not one hundred per cent capable at the moment – but he didn't want to abandon his men to the fraught ork-hunt through the corridors of the battleship.

'I'll coordinate the purge from here, sir,' Shaffenbeck said, reading the conflict in his superior's expression. 'Get back to the bridge where you can do the most good.'

'Very well,' Kulik replied gratefully. 'Keep an eye out, I don't want to have to go looking for another officer, do you hear? Sergeant Latheram, I commend your bravery but I am also ordering you and all other wounded to report to the surgeon's halls. Call in more men once the flight decks have been secured, Mister Shaffenbeck.'

The armsman sergeant looked about to argue, but thought better of it and accepted his captain's command with a stiff salute, the action of which sent a ripple of pain across his face. Two men stepped up to helped their injured leader but he waved them away and started off aft under his own power.

'You know,' said Shaffenbeck, watching the sergeant leave, 'with men like that, we might just win this damned battle.'

Kulik was too tired to admonish Saul for his cursing. He pushed himself upright, sheathed his sword and holstered his pistol. Straightening his coat and his back with equal effort, the captain started back towards the bridge. Medical orderlies were coming down the corridor and he gave them a nod of appreciation as he passed.

Action shaped thought, and by acting reserved and disciplined some of Kulik's calm had returned by the time he was back at the bridge. The adrenal rush of the hack and slay of combat was ebbing away, but as he had told Shaffenbeck, they were nowhere near the end of this fight yet.

The bridge doors groaned open in front of Kulik and he stepped back onto the command deck. It took him a moment to adjust from the frenzied shouts and sweaty gore of hand-to-hand combat, to the rhythmic chatter of servitors and the soft exchanges of the bridge crew. Behind the armoured doors seemed a different world and Kulik felt almost dizzy with the dissonance. He was brought back to focus by Price.

'Ah, there you are, captain. I hope you enjoyed yourself disposing of our unwanted guests.'

'It's being dealt with.' Kulik took in a sharp breath. 'Admiral.'

The captain assumed his usual position and passed a quick eye over every screen and console. The ork ships with the teleporters had been destroyed and the squadron of cruisers assisting *Colossus* had broken through the orks. Three cruisers were crippled and that many again destroyed from the flotilla. The rest of the rimward fleet was not quite so badly mauled, having had extra time to respond to the ork ruse. The coreward flotilla, which made up the starboard axis of the attack, was almost unscathed. The patrol flotilla ships were now in a position to turn back and trap a large part of the ork fleet against the main line of the rimward fleet. Price seemed to be in the middle of ordering the relief attack, and half the flotilla had already started the manoeuvre.

'Communication from the flagship, captain,' reported Lieutenant Hartnell.

'Accept transmission,' Kulik replied, crossing his arms.

A sub-screen enlarged, filled with the static of a vid-comm burst. The face of Lord High Admiral Lansung glared down at the men on the bridge.

'What are you turning around for, Price?' Lansung demanded. 'The route to the ork star base is open. You will rendezvous with Commodore Semmes and continue the attack without delay. That is my command.'

Price stepped back as if struck, brow knotted. He signalled for the comms officer to switch to transmission.

'This is Admiral Price. If we abandon the rimward fleet now, they will suffer badly at the hands of the orks. They're taking on pretty much all of the enemy on their own at the moment. We must provide assistance.'

The admiral turned away and started to pace while he waited for a reply. Kulik stopped him at one end of his perambulations.

'Sir, I think the Lord High Admiral is right,' the captain admitted. 'We have to push home the advantage while the attack moon is virtually unguarded. The orks have been trying to keep us away from the base as hard as they can, and I don't think it's as invulnerable as they want us to believe. The flight wings of the *Colossus* are needed for the attack, along with the rest of the carrier group.'

Before Price could answer, Lansung's message arrived through the aether. He looked calm, but his voice was edged with rage.

'Admiral Price, I have given you a direct order. *Colossus* and all attendant ships are to join the attack on the ork star fort. Failure to obey will be mutiny.'

'Ignore him,' snapped Price. 'Continue to come about.'

'Belay that!' Kulik felt Price's glare like a slap across the face and flushed red with shame, but there was no other option. 'Admiral, we must obey and join the attack.'

'Officer of the watch, have the armsmen attend to the bridge and place Captain Kulik in custody. He is under arrest for insubordination.'

'Belay that order,' growled Kulik. The officers around the bridge looked on, horrified as they watched their two commanders arguing. The captain laid his hand on the hilt of his sword and stared at Price. He was shaking, scared more by this confrontation than by the bloody fight with the greenskins. 'This is my ship, admiral, and I have received a direct order from the Lord High Admiral. You will remove yourself from my bridge and remain in your quarters until such time as you have recovered your composure.'

Price bridled, lip quivering with indignation. Kulik leaned closer and dropped his voice to a whisper.

'For the sake of the men, do not require me to summon the armsmen, sir. Let us act like officers.'

Kulik's words seemed to strike a chord somewhere in the admiral's mind and a hint of realisation crept into his expression. He nodded mutely, confused, and then shook his head. Kulik thought Price was going to argue again, but the admiral's shoulders slumped in defeat.

'I... I am feeling... indisposed, Captain Kulik. I think it better if I retire to my cabin at this juncture. I do not feel well at all.'

'That would be for the best,' Kulik replied gently. 'I will have the surgeon send an orderly with something relaxing for you. Mister Crassock, please assist the admiral to his quarters.'

Price nodded dumbly once more, looking every bit the old man he was becoming, frail and uncertain. Kulik could not understand what had happened to his mentor, his friend, and it cut him deep to see Ensign Crassock helping Price off the command deck. When the door closed behind them, Kulik drove the image from his thoughts.

'Signal to fleet. All vessels to make all speed possible to the flagship for immediate attack on the objective.'

Kulik realised he was still holding the hilt of his sword, his knuckles white with strain. He released his grip and flexed his fingers, forcing himself to relax. Emperor protect me, he thought, from orks and admirals.

EIGHTEEN

Terra – the Imperial Palace

On past occasions Wienand had lamented the sheep-like mentality of humanity, and in particular their desire to crowd onto Terra in their tens of thousands to pay homage to the God-Emperor of Mankind. Even amongst the Inquisition such thoughts were becoming heretical, but Wienand had read the ancient records and knew, or at least had a semi-educated inkling, just how 'godly' the Emperor was. There were some, like Veritus, who had embraced the teachings of the Ecclesiarchy and openly supported the organisation. Wienand remained unconvinced of the necessity for an Imperium-spanning church, but she could certainly see that it might have its uses.

At the moment its greatest use came in the form of a queue five miles long, winding back and forth up the Avenue of Martyrs towards the Cathedral of the Saviour Emperor. Having cut and double-backed through the crowds at the transit station several times to confuse any potential pursuer, eventually emerging out of the southern gate, Wienand had plunged straight into the milling tide of humanity.

Amongst the press of bodies, the inquisitor found herself inside a sort of mobile shanty. It took days, weeks usually, for anyone wishing to enter the Cathedral itself to achieve this, and such was the demand that it then took another three days to process from the massive doors to the entrance of the inner basilica where the altar could be seen. Each pilgrim had roughly three seconds in the presence of the relics kept in stasis there before being moved on by armed Frateris. It seemed an awful lot of effort to see a couple of metal shards – supposedly from the Emperor's armour – and a pile of ash that was once, so the Ministorum claimed, a fragment of Roboute Guilliman's cloak.

People had tents, handwagons and portable cooking stoves, gathered as families, groups and even entire communities that had made the long and arduous journey to the heart of the Imperium. Most of them, even those that had been considered wealthy when departing, would have expended their every resource to chart passage. Some would have worked their way from system to system, haphazardly crossing the stars, edging ever closer to their destination.

There were clothes and fashions from thousands of different worlds. Underhive punks with extravagant gang hairstyles and tattoos who had been touched by the light of the Emperor queued meekly alongside labourers in heavy coveralls and hand-woven smocks. Various individuals of planetary nobilities moved serenely through the mass atop sedan chairs carried by augmented servants, or cut themselves off inside servitor-pulled wains covered with brilliantly embroidered panels and sheets. No powered vehicles, save for the patrol transports of the Adeptus Arbites, were allowed on the Avenue of Martyrs, nor animals, so all transportation was either on foot or man-powered in some fashion.

A middle-aged couple had procured quadcycles and were gently pedalling in fits and starts as the queue edged forwards, their teenage offspring riding on top of the trailers hitched behind. Wienand suspected that both parents and children had been a lot younger when their pilgrimage had begun.

Quite a few were recognisable as ex-military: Guardsmen and Naval personnel who had earned the right to pilgrimage by conquest or bravery. That right might bring them to Terra but it didn't extend so far as jumping the queue. Conversely, the western edge of the roadway was reserved solely for members of the Ecclesiarchy. Preachers and missionaries with letters of reference from cardinals of recognised dioceses were granted access, alongside a few fortunate individuals of the Frateris who had earned similar reward for services rendered. Amongst the cassocks, uniforms and robes were ornately dressed members of higher-class families, whose dedication to the Adeptus Ministorum had perhaps been more financial than physical or spiritual.

There were growls of annoyance and accusing shouts as Wienand pushed herself through the mass, suspected of trying to jump her place. A few brave souls made grabs and lunges but were soon dissuaded from further action by a flash of her bolt pistol; the Inquisition sigil of the ring on her trigger finger was even more of a deterrent for many.

Anyone who had spent more than five minutes on Terra learned to keep an eye out for the stylised 'I' with cross-bars, and to affect an air of total disinterest in anybody that possessed such a thing.

She continued to worm her way through the throng. It was hard to chart any kind of course. Not only was the press of people like a thicket, allowing passage in some places and obstinately blocking it in others, great incense burners hung from the ceiling above the Avenue of Martyrs. The smoke from these spilled down like a fog, obscuring visibility even further. Wienand was dimly aware of the tenements rising up on either side of the vast thoroughfare, storey after storey of small cell windows, broken by the occasional spray of stained glass where the way-chapels were situated.

Peddlers of all descriptions moved up and down between the columns of the pilgrimage queue. Their wares ranged from the mundane to the extraordinary. Many were selling food and clothes, others had small trinkets and keepsakes purportedly from the Cathedral itself. Quite a few were soil-men, with synth-leather bottles and buckets and brightly painted portable screens to allow the pilgrims to relieve themselves without losing their place; those that were prepared made their own arrangements or organised themselves into queuing shifts to avoid such expense. There were several touting out their services as place-holders. They would, for the right fee, happily queue in place of a pilgrim so that they might spend a day or two resting in one of the dorm cells or perhaps visit one of the lesser attractions of the Imperial Palace.

More exotic were the modified queue-folk. Wienand spied

a tele-bless. The woman's eyes had been replaced with optical lenses and the bulky, cable-pierced box of a storage drive jutted from the side of her skull. She had been inside the holy sepulchre of the Cathedral and was willing to allow others to access her sights and memories for the right price, thus passing on the holiness of the sanctuary without the irksome waiting.

Messenger cherubs – vat-grown winged creatures with angelic faces and dead eyes – flitted back and forth through the haze of incense above the milling crowd, carrying missives to and from the Cathedral offices. She decided to follow their course to keep her bearing as the crowd surged and rippled around her, edging ever closer to unity with the Emperor.

Although the mass of pilgrims gave her plenty of cover in which to hide, it also prevented Wienand from seeing if she was still being pursued. She was sure that whoever had followed her down the tunnel would have been close enough to track her progress into the multitude, and if they were in communication with others sworn to Veritus and his allies she might well be at the centre of a converging net.

She needed to get into the hab-blocks, effect a change of clothes – and preferably dye her hair – before disappearing altogether. Over the heads of the throng around her the inquisitor could see the top of an arched entrance to the nearest hab-block, about three hundred feet away. She started to head towards it, stepping past an elderly couple who had sat down on the ferrocrete with a small stove to brew a pot of some hot beverage or other. They were dressed in mendicant robes – undyed smocks given out for those that needed to sell the last of their belongings, including their clothes, for food and water.

'Tai, dear?' asked the old lady, offering up a much-chipped ceramic cup and saucer. 'You seem in an awful hurry. Why not relax a moment and have a nice cup of tai?'

Wienand couldn't help but grin at the lady's attitude. To keep a tai set whilst dressed in charity rags demonstrated an adherence to a certain level of standards that gave Wienand a momentary lift in spirits.

'No, thank you, but I appreciate the offer,' said Wienand. She delved into a secret pocket inside her jacket and produced a brassy coin. On one side was the Inquisitorial symbol and on the other her personal mark. She handed the token to the old man and pointed to an Adeptus Arbites watch-tower about half a mile ahead. 'When you get to the way-station, show them this. Say that Inquisitor Wienand instructs that they escort you to the front of the queue.'

The couple looked at her wide-eyed, caught between shock and fear. Wienand winked and turned away.

At that moment she saw a commotion in the crowd about a dozen feet ahead of her. Someone was bulldozing their way through the pilgrims straight towards Wienand, smashing aside people in their haste.

With surprised shouts and angry yells the crowd parted, revealing a well-muscled man bulging out of the seams of a mendicant robe. The hood was thrown back as he sprinted towards her; he had an ageing, broad face with a squashed nose, and his bald scalp was crossed with three faint scars.

Wienand dragged free her bolt pistol but her attacker was shockingly fast and she did not have time to aim before he had reached her – she could not risk a wild shot with so many others around. The man's hands were empty of weapons, she realised, and an out-thrust palm struck Wienand in the chest, hurling her back several yards, crashing through the brew set of the old couple, skidding and rolling across the rough ferrocrete.

The old man gave a shout, of pain rather than surprise, and lurched to his feet clutching his shoulder. Blood spurted between his fingers as he staggered a few steps and fell down to his knees.

Only here, as she lay on her back, did Wienand realise what was happening. The man's face flashed from a memory of Rendenstein's reports: Esad Wire, known as Beast Krule. It seemed that Vangorich was making his own play.

However, in the next instant she happened to look up and saw what it was that the Beast had also seen. In one of the hab windows on the far side of the avenue, about five hundred feet away, light glinted from a lens of some kind. Probably a telescopic gunsight.

Wienand rolled to her right out of pure instinct a moment before the sniper fired again, the high-velocity bullet cracking from the roadway where she had been moments before. Still dazed, Wienand did not resist when Beast Krule snatched the bolt pistol from her hand and turned towards the firer. There was something about his pose, the set of his shoulders and legs, the raw sturdiness of the man, which suggested some kind of endoskeletal bracing.

Beast Krule fired back at the sniper, a salvo of three bolts. From this range Wienand would have thought the shot impossible, but the trio of bolts arced over the crowd and dropped into the window. Krule had some kind of optical imaging and had even allowed for the decay rate of the bolts' internal propellant. The flash of detonations illuminated a gaunt, shocked face within the dorm cell.

Wienand rolled to her feet, pulling free her laspistol. Other figures were converging on them from the crowd. Some of the pilgrims were rooted in horror, others were screaming, while many were trying to push their way back into the packed throng, trying to get away. The old woman had crawled over to her husband and was cradling him in her arms, a patch of wet red spreading through the crude grey weave of her smock.

'Watch out!' Wienand's warning came just in time as a woman in a dark red Imperial Guard uniform lunged from the crowd at Krule, her hand clutching a gleaming power sword. The Assassin turned just in time, the shimmering blade slicing through the folds of the robe around his neck but missing flesh. Krule snapped out his right hand, fingers extended. The woman's throat disappeared in a welter of foaming blood.

Another assailant dressed in the same manner, tall and lean, erupted from the panicked people to Wienand's right. The inquisitor fired and there was a flash of light as a conversion field absorbed the energy of the las-shot. She didn't have time for another, but Krule was there again, a kick snapping the legs from under the man, shattering shin bones. The Beast was on top of him in moments, driving reinforced fists through his chest and ribs.

Someone barrelled into Wienand from behind. She squirmed and twisted as she fell, firing the laspistol point-blank into the person's gut. Hot breath warmed the inquisitor's neck as the two of them hit the ground hard, forcing the air out of Wienand's lungs. She stared into the red lenses of a pair of bionic eyes inches from her face, and was distantly aware of a sharp pain just above her right hip.

Suddenly the weight on Wienand was lifted away. The man seemed to rise into the air, blood drops falling from the blade of the long knife in his left hand, a scorch mark on the flak armour covering his torso beneath the layers of a preacher's vestments. At first Wienand thought it was Krule who threw her assailant a dozen feet, but the robed, hooded figure was too slender. Her saviour stooped down, extending a hand with well-manicured fingernails and a small tattoo of a skull between thumb and index finger that Wienand recognised immediately.

'Rendenstein? I knew you were alive!'

Wienand's aide nodded inside the hood and stepped past, delivering a skull-smashing punch to a man swinging a maul at Beast Krule's exposed back. The Assassin reared up, bloodied hands flinging gore. He spun around but stopped himself as he pulled back his right fist.

'That's the last of them,' growled Vangorich's agent. He looked at Rendenstein and his eyes widened. 'That I know of. There'll be more soon, ma'am. We should go.'

'Arbitrators!' snapped Wienand, spying a knot of blue-armoured enforcers with shock shields and power mauls shouldering their way through the crowd a few dozen feet away. 'This is no time for answering awkward questions!'

Krule led the way and Rendenstein took the rear, Wienand wedged protectively between the two enhanced warriors.

They headed away from the incoming Arbitrators and found the shelter of an arched entranceway to one of the transit tenements.

Krule hit the steps inside at a run, going up two floors before turning along one of the landings and sprinting along its length to another stairwell, where he ascended again. Wienand wasn't sure if he was heading somewhere specific or simply navigating at random, but after five minutes of hard running that had the inquisitor's heart thrashing in her chest and her lungs burning, the Assassin finally came to a stop beside the open door of a pilgrim cell. He stepped inside and reappeared a moment later.

Wienand was almost doubled up, choking down huge gulps of air. She hadn't realised the price her body had paid for the past few years being dormant on Terra. Rendenstein stepped past to guard the other side of the doorway, her skin as porcelain-like as usual. Krule glanced at the inquisitor's aide with a look of appreciation before concentrating on Wienand.

'All clear, ma'am,' said Beast, taking Wienand by the arm and leading her into the room. It was a bare chamber about ten feet square, with a low pallet bed in one corner, a washstand with rusted taps in another and a bedside table in which had been left a tattered copy of the *Lectitio Divinatus*. 'Sit down, let's take a look at that cut.'

Wienand complied, wincing as her clothes pulled at the dried blood forming a scab over her hip. Rendenstein eased Krule aside, concerned for her mistress. The Assassin stepped away and glanced out of the narrow window before he pulled the thin rag of a curtain across.

'I think I'm missing a few pieces of this puzzle,' said Wienand, looking between Krule and Rendenstein.

Both Assassin and assistant started to talk at the same time and then stopped. They looked at each other with embarrassed smiles. Krule waved for Rendenstein to begin again.

'Your unscheduled and unpublicised meeting with Grand Master Vangorich meant that you were not in your chambers as expected when Veritus' men came for you,' said the bodyguard-aide.

'You're sure they're from Veritus?' asked Wienand.

'Positive. I was compiling records on known agents on Terra of those inquisitors taking part in the conclave. I recognised one of them. They must have realised I had guessed why they were there. I killed one and managed to get away.'

'I was following you from when you were finished with the Grand Master, ma'am,' continued Krule. 'I did a quick sweep of your offices after you left–'

'I thought I locked down the whole area?' said Wienand.

Krule shrugged apologetically and continued.

'I saw what you had come across, but by the time I reached the shuttle platform you had already departed. I had to follow you along the track. I was trying to catch up, but you were moving too quickly. Once you hit the public spaces I didn't want to draw attention to myself in case I drew attention to you as well. When I spotted the sniper, I had to act.'

'And I ended up following Krule, though he didn't realise it,' said Rendenstein. 'I started on the eastbound shuttle to the transport hub, but jumped off a few hundred yards into the tunnel to lose my pursuers. I didn't know you would be returning – sorry it wasn't there for you when you came to the monorail. After that I went to check your personal quarters and found another one of our attackers there. I was too late to save Aemelie, but I killed him before he could get away. The bodies are stashed in the maintenance ducts. I was returning to the offices when I heard footsteps. I hid for a few minutes and that's when I heard the other carriage being started. I hurried back, expecting it to be you, just in time to see Krule chasing you into the tunnels.'

'And here we all are...' said Wienand. 'Veritus sent his thugs to kill me at the offices, then at my apartments, and then chased me to the Cathedral. They seem very keen to silence me.'

She gasped as Rendenstein peeled away her blood-matted shirt to reveal a narrow but deep stab wound in her side.

'I've seen worse,' said Krule.

'You've inflicted worse,' replied Rendenstein. Wienand thought she detected a hint of admiration in her bodyguard's tone and expression. 'But you're right. No major internal injury, no arteries or organs damaged.'

'Amateurs,' muttered Beast, twitching the curtain to glance outside again. He looked back at Wienand. 'So what should we do now, ma'am?'

Wienand was at a loss. Stage one was a success. She had survived. Barely. Stage two would be to counter Veritus' plans to usurp power in the Senatorum Imperialis. Wienand was going to have to call in a lot of favours and the whole matter would surely send shockwaves through the Inquisition. This was potentially a very divisive moment and she would have to handle it carefully. Even if Veritus was beyond caring about the repercussions of his actions – a self-righteousness Wienand had witnessed in other long-serving inquisitors too – she did not want to fracture the very organisation that would be needed at its most united in this time of peril.

'Aemelie,' said Rendenstein.

'What of her?' asked Wienand.

'Who is Aemelie?' said Krule.

'My body-double,' Wienand told him. 'Aemelie is my surgical doppelganger for certain occasions. What about her?'

'She's dead, not much use now,' said Rendenstein. 'I hid her body with that of the man who killed her.'

'And we can use her to make Veritus think I'm dead too,' said Wienand, catching up on her aide's train of thought. The inquisitor looked at Krule. 'Do you think you could recover the corpses and stage them to look like it was me?'

'I'm sure I can manage something, ma'am,' said Krule. He looked at Rendenstein with a hopeful expression. 'If I had some help, things would go more smoothly.'

'Stay here and rest,' said Rendenstein, looking at Wienand, 'and I'll bring back medicae supplies to fix that for you.'

'Very well,' said Wienand. 'I'll also need to change my appearance. Something cosmetic will do for the moment, we'll worry about fingerprints and gene-trackers later.'

Wienand took a deep breath and looked solemnly at her companions.

'Time that I died.'

NINETEEN

Port Sanctus – inner system

Glory or death.

It was the unofficial motto of the Imperial Navy and Lord High Admiral Lansung had evidently taken it to heart. The head of the entire Navy was going to return to Terra in triumph or he was going to ensure nobody returned at all.

The *Colossus* ploughed across the void along with the other launch-capable ships that had broken through the ork line. Behind the spearpoint formed by the carrier task-force came the other battleships and cruisers.

Lansung's approach – it would be stretching the word 'plan' – was brutally simple. The flight wings – bombers, fighters and assault boats – would precede the main attack fleet with a single massive wave of craft. Intelligence suggested the attack moon's gravitic manipulation was not advanced enough to target the small attack craft. They were to inflict as much damage as possible, hopefully disabling the gravity beam weapons and shielding, leaving the attack moon vulnerable to conventional weapons.

It was a long shot, Kulik knew, and the battleship's captain suspected that Lansung knew it too. It was an all-or-nothing gamble that would cost the lives of many men, and see the destruction of many ships, even if they were successful.

Such was the price of victory.

Such was the sacrifice required to bring some hope to the defenders of the Imperium in their dark hour. If such hope needed to be watered with the blood of the Imperial Navy, Lansung was willing to shed an ocean of it.

In his heart Kulik knew the Lord High Admiral was mostly concerned with his own reputation and position. There could be no denying Lansung's more selfish qualities. Against that, the captain weighed up what he knew of the Imperial Navy. He believed that no matter what Lansung did, or what the Lord High Admiral desired for himself, the Navy was an honourable and good organisation. Even the likes of Acharya and Price, men who reckoned pride and reputation higher than obedience and brotherhood, had in them an intrinsic quality imbued by the best traditions of the Imperial Navy.

It took a peculiar and particular sort of man or woman to command a starship. In defeat, death was almost certain. Unlike the Imperial Guard officer, the Navy lieutenant and captain rarely had opportunity to retreat or regroup. Reinforcements were very rarely on hand. Independence of thought had to be chained to rigid discipline, for years at a time could pass without contact with higher authority. Only a man or woman absolutely committed and self-confident could ever hope to tame the beast that was a warship.

It was no surprise that there were those who fell prey to

hubris and arrogance. To be a captain of a cruiser or battle-ship was to hold absolute power over the lives of thousands of men and women. Power could corrupt, and in Lansung's case it certainly had. But at the start, many years ago, even Lansung had been a fresh-faced officer stepping aboard a starship for the first time.

No matter how cynical or vain that young officer must have been, Kulik believed that even the most selfish and hardened heart could not be totally immune to the romance and glory of the Imperial Navy. Young Lansung had dreamed of honour and prizes and perhaps fame. Kulik believed – had to believe, for his universe to have any mean-ing at all – that there was still an iota of that young officer somewhere deep inside Lansung. If he did not think that, it would be impossible for the captain to lay down his life, and the lives of his crew, upon the altar of the man's ambition.

The ships of the Imperial Navy cruised towards the attack moon. The ork star base lived up to its namesake in size, being several hundred miles across, though in shape this particular example was more rectangular than others. Mile-high outcroppings speared from its crater-pocked sur-face and with the scanners on maximum Kulik could see that it had probably once been an actual moon of some kind. Like the rock forts, it had been mined from the inside out, creating a vast network of caverns within its interior.

A few ork ships had turned around to chase the Impe-rial vessels back towards their base but these were easily held off by squadrons of frigates and destroyers. The ships of the line formed up into their battlegroups while the car-rier force plunged ahead.

Kulik felt his breath coming shorter, his chest tight as his flotilla sped on towards the attack moon. It defied belief – had not similar creations all across the outer Segmentum Solar devastated systems, ravaged fleets and wiped out whole worlds?

He suddenly felt ridiculous, charging towards the immense battle station like some knight of old charging at a hive city with a lance. Kulik swallowed hard and looked at Shaffenbeck.

The first lieutenant was back at his customary place, having handed over leadership of the ork hunt to Lieutenant Hartley. Kulik was glad to have his second close at hand. The lieutenant was fixed on the screen too, hands clasped behind his back, knuckles whitening from the pressure. He sensed his captain's attention and shot a glance at his superior that conveyed a mixture of dread and fatalism.

The best traditions of the Imperial Navy, thought Kulik. We don't show it but everyone on this bridge, everyone on this ship, is quietly terrified. We tame it like the plasma in a reactor, channelling that fear into discipline and courage.

There was a deeper sensation than mere fear for his life working in Kulik's gut. The greater part of the fleet was here, attacking a single ork moon. If they failed not only would Port Sanctus be lost, it would signal that the orks' stations were impervious to the Imperium's counter-attacks. He stepped closer to Saul as he considered that this battle signified the future of mankind. Failure here meant the orks would probably not be stopped. Never. Even if they were halted in one final battle, the rest of the Imperium would be drained dry of resources, ships and soldiers from other segmentuns drawn from their duties to combat the rampaging greenskins. Even if Terra held – as it had held in the Heresy War – the rest of the Imperium would fall prey to renegades, eldar, and sundry other dangers that threatened the existence of mankind's dominions every day.

Glory or death.

Not at all. This was raw, primal battle for survival against one of the primeval forces of the galaxy. It was a test of the Emperor's servants. If they could not crush the orks they did not deserve to rule the galaxy.

It was not long before the lead elements of the fleet came within range of the attack moon's gravitic pulses. Strange arcs of green and blue energy flashed between ramshackle pylons studding the base's surface. Their pulsing matched Kulik's breathing, quickening with the passing seconds.

Like the mass ejections of a star this energy lashed outwards across the void, spitting green fire and flame, twisting the fabric of space-time around the fronds of energy. Kulik could not suppress a grimace and there came cries of dismay across the bridge as the *Heartless Rogue* was engulfed by a tendril of power, which seemed to wrap around the heavy cruiser like a tentacle. Impossible forces constricted, crushing the ship as void shields turned into red lightning, crumpling yards-thick hull like paper until the reactor containment fields ruptured and the heavy cruiser was swallowed by an expanding ball of plasma.

The corona of energy that had surrounded the moon dissipated, expended by the gravity-warping lash. Kulik had no idea how long it would take to recharge, but realised there was a window of opportunity to get close enough for the launch before the devastating weapon could be unleashed again.

It was a slim hope, but he was prepared to grasp anything that would make this seem like less of a suicide mission.

'*Colossus*, this is *Agamemnon*,' came a transmission on vox-only. 'We are preparing to launch.'

'Not yet, *Agamemnon*,' Kulik replied swiftly, the order issued with gritted teeth. He knew that Nadelin didn't want to get any closer to the attack moon; none of them did. But they had to put their heads into the dragon's mouth if they were going to rip out its guts. 'We have to all be within launch range and send the attack craft as a single wing. If we do this piecemeal they'll be picked off before they ever reach their targets.'

'Negative, *Colossus*. We can't risk getting that close. That gravity whip will tear us apart!'

'Damn it, Captain Nadelin, you will follow orders!' Kulik snatched the comms pick-up from the arm of his command throne and his voice dropped to an angry whisper. 'Emperor help me, Nadelin, if I see you launching your wings now I'll blow you out of the stars myself!'

There was no reply, but the *Agamemnon* continued on course a few hundred miles ahead of the *Colossus* and showed no signs of slowing for a launch.

More conventional weapons opened fire from batteries cut into the surface of the attack moon and turrets mounted on the jutting edifices. Shells and energy beams spewed across the void, too far for any kind of accuracy.

'I do think they might be worried, sir,' Saul said. 'They're trying to scare us off!'

'You might be right, Mister Shaffenbeck,' said Kulik.

They were only a few thousand miles from optimum range when the crackling field of gravitic energy plumed outwards from the pylons again.

'Emperor's arse,' muttered Shaffenbeck as a green tendril of fire filled the vid-display, seeming to head directly for the *Colossus*.

'Don't blaspheme,' said Kulik. He winced as the display was filled with the static of the energy surge.

The gravity lash hit *Agamemnon* and *Crusading Ire*, tearing apart both ships like the shoddily-made toys of some enraged infant. Debris was scattered across the void, clouds of gases and rupturing corpses sprayed over the heavens as if by the hand of an uncaring alien god. *Colossus'* void shields flared from the backwash but the battleship plunged through the expanding debris field unscathed.

'Launch all wings!' bellowed Kulik. 'Signal to flotilla, all attack wings to launch now! Let's get our pilots away before that thing is ready to fire again.'

The batteries and laser cannons were starting to find their mark as a dozen warships spewed wave after wave of aircraft from their launch bays. Glittering like ice, the attack craft sped across the void towards the ork star fort. Those ships capable of launching torpedoes added such ordnance to the mass of objects flying towards the attack moon. Turning broadside on to their target, the carrier craft formed a standard line of battle, their turrets and gun decks responding to the fire coming from the greenskins. Void shields burned bright and power fields protecting the attack moon flared with spits of orange and red.

Lansung and the main battle line were committed to the attack. There was no time to wait to see if the bomber wings were successful, so dozens of Imperial ships forged ahead, engines trailing plasma across the blackness of space. The *Autocephalax Eternal* led the charge, the bright gold of her eagle-headed prow gleaming in the light of the system's star. Vessel after vessel followed the massive flagship, the schematic of the strategic display so crowded with identifier runes that it was a mass of incomprehensible blue.

The gravity whips powered up again before the first wings had reached their target. Kulik realised that *Colossus* was now the closest ship. He watched with morbid fascination as coils of energy coruscated up the pylons, building in intensity. The captain turned to his second-in-command and spoke quietly.

'This is very likely going to destroy us, Saul,' said Kulik. It took every effort to sound conversational. No stranger to battle, Kulik was nevertheless convinced for the first time ever that this was the end. The attack moon was too powerful. The orks were too powerful.

'Very likely, Rafal,' replied the lieutenant.

'If I am to die I would like to go to the Emperor knowing one thing.'

'What is that?'

'Why did you never take your captain's exam?'

Saul laughed, long and hard; so long that Kulik feared the attack moon would rip them to pieces before he had his answer. After what seemed like an age, the first lieutenant composed himself enough to reply.

'I can't stand to take another exam, sir. Captain Astersom,

he terrified me at my lieutenant's exam. I mean, actually terrified me. I wanted to kill myself. The thought of going through that again, the fear of failure, the scorn, the worry… I'd rather face a hundred attack moons than another board of examination.'

'That's it?' Kulik was not sure if he was relieved or disappointed. He turned his attention back to the alien base filling the screen. The energy flow was almost at the tips of the pylons and sparks were starting to fly between the jagged metal spires. He looked back at Shaffenbeck. 'Really, that's it?'

Saul shrugged.

Kulik almost cried out in surprise when the first torpedo hit the surface of the attack moon. A cluster of warheads tore apart one of the pylons, causing green energy to flare outwards in an uncontrolled burst that spat uselessly past the approaching bomber wings.

More torpedoes hit home, though most impacted harmlessly onto the rocky surface of the base, creating fresh craters but doing little else. Close-range defence weapons opened fire with bolts of laser and streams of tracer shells as the Imperial Navy aircraft dived down towards the attack moon's exposed gun batteries and turrets. Blossoms of incendiary and high-explosive fire raked across bunker-like extrusions and detonated inside yawning caves that scarred the base's outer crust. More wicked green fire spewed in all directions, slapping aside a squadron of Cobra destroyers like a man swatting flies, four ships turned into slag and plasma in a few seconds by the writhing energy plume.

The *Colossus* poured out what fire it could with the rest of the carrier flotilla, until the flagship and the rest of Lansung's fleet arrived. Nova cannons and mass drivers, cyclonic and atomic torpedoes, plasma blasts and melta-missiles ravaged the attack moon as ship after ship closed in, unleashed its fury and then turned away, broadsides thundering as the line passed through the manoeuvre.

Kulik did not think it was going to be enough, even the combined firepower of half the segmentum fleet. Void shields overloaded under the barrage of shells and torrent of energy bolts disgorged by the attack moon's fury. Half a dozen cruisers were broken in half by sporadic flails of the gravity whip while huge rockets and crackling particle accelerators tore apart the battleships *Restitution* and *Almighty Deliverance*, their void shield detonations sending out shockwaves that batted attack craft across the ether.

Kulik saw something in the depths of the attack moon. A green glow was brightening from within, starting to gleam out of launch bays and vision ports. He saw the flit of fighters and bombers silhouetted against the light, inside the ork base. The pilots were guiding their craft into the heart of the star fort, no doubt sacrificing themselves to launch their attacks against the unprotected innards of the gravitic generators.

'That's going to overload, sir,' said Shaffenbeck.

Kulik didn't know whether to laugh or cry. They were going to destroy an attack moon! Whether they would survive or not, he was not sure. Lansung must have felt the same.

'General order to fleet, withdraw with all speed, captain,' announced the comms officer.

'Helm, you heard the command,' snapped Kulik.

'What about our pilots, sir?' Shaffenbeck asked quietly. Kulik suppressed a swallow of regret and silently shook his head. 'Understood, sir.'

The last ships of the fleet were still making their attack runs when the star fort exploded. Its detonation tore a rent through space-time, engulfing half a dozen more capital ships with fronds of lethal energy, swallowing escorts, bombers and fighters whole. For a moment Kulik thought he heard a roar of pain, an outburst of primal anguish that clawed into the back of his head and twisted like a fist around his thoughts.

Then the outer edge of the shockwave caught up with the *Colossus*.

TWENTY

Terra – the Imperial Palace

Fanfare did not begin to describe the conditions that greeted Admiral Lansung's arrival. Pomp, ceremony, spectacle. Even these words would not convey the massive grandeur, the overbearing ostentation and carnival that engulfed the chambers of the Senatorum Imperialis as the minutes counted down to the arrival of the Lord High Admiral's gun cutter.

The Praetorian Way, which curved gently along the shoulder of a mountain from the Eastgate landing hall to a grandiose gatehouse, was lined by a thousand Lucifer Blacks in full armour on one side, and a thousand Naval armsmen on the other. Every tenth man bore a banner of title, naming a battle victory of the Imperial Navy. Behind both lines were trumpeters, drummers, hornsmen, chanters and chantresses. The instruments broke out into heady anthemic life, the voices of the choristers raised against the wind that blew across the Praetorian Way and snapped the flags atop the towers that reared above the proceedings.

Sparkling with gilded decoration, the gun cutter descended. The effect must have been engineered, somehow, thought Vangorich as he watched the display from the entrance to the Senatorum Imperialis halls. The usual layer of mist around the peak from which Eastgate was partially built had been dispersed, as had the clouds that dominated the skies above the Imperial Palace. That in itself was no small endeavour, all for the vanity of one man.

Around and in front of Vangorich stood the other High Lords. The past two weeks had been a fraught time, for the Senatorum in general and for Vangorich in particular. Wienand had gone missing, as had her aide-bodyguard and Beast Krule, who had been tailing her. There were a few whispers from within the Inquisition that Wienand had been found dead in her quarters, her corpse next to that of her attacker. Vangorich did not hold out any hope for his own operative, though he wondered what force Wienand's enemies possessed that could best an experienced inquisitor and two of the most augmented warriors on Terra. The prospect of confronting such power unsettled Vangorich enough to stifle any opposition he might voice against the appointment of Wienand's successor.

It was fear of the unknown – the enemy Vangorich hated above all others – that had curbed the Grand Master's plans. The Senatorum had been convened and Lord Veritus had quickly established himself as the new Inquisitorial Representative. His first declaration to the High Lords was that there would be inquisitors coming to Terra to look into all of the dealings of the Senatorum and its members, starting with the Officio Assassinorum.

It was a clever move. It caused outrage, of course, that the Inquisition should impugn the honour of the noble High Lords, but the selection of the Assassins as the first target served a double purpose. Firstly, the other High Lords were largely united in their dislike for Vangorich and his organisation, and to see both humbled in this manner made the senators feel better. Secondly, it gave them notice to hide or destroy such records as needed to go missing; a tacit agreement between the Senatorum and the Inquisition that things were going to change but the High Lords would keep their heads as long as they had the decency to hide the evidence well and stop whatever it was they knew they had been doing wrong.

Lansung, being physically removed from this burgeoning purge, had suffered neither the wrath of Veritus nor the more insidious doubts that had followed the Inquisitorial Representative's pronouncements. In a way it was just what the Senatorum needed; enlightened self-interest had fallen by the wayside in the face of the orks, but Veritus had brought back the dog-eat-dog politics that allowed the Senatorum to function properly, if not efficiently.

Vangorich glanced at the man himself, standing a few feet to the Assassin's right. His stark powered suit was in the shadow of the great entrance arch, his face lit from beneath by the glow of the collar lamps, giving Veritus an even gaunter, draconian appearance. It was a powerful image; one that Vangorich filed away for possible future use. The Grand Master could barely believe that Veritus had turned up to his first Senatorum session in full armour, but the effect had not been lost on the other High Lords. Delving deeper, Vangorich had come to understand that the suit acted as a life support system as well as personal protection. Already schemes were in motion to find out if Veritus ever left the confines of that armour.

The trumpeting, drumming and singing reached a crescendo, causing Vangorich to look along the length of the Praetorian Way to the twin landing spars of Eastgate. Lansung's cutter, still magically gleaming, touched down on the upper of the two pads. From this distance, more than half a mile away, only small shapes could be made out as the Lord High Admiral descended from the cutter and boarded an open-topped ground-skimmer.

The only news that had reached Terra concerning the admiral's exploits had arrived two days earlier. Evidently Lansung's flagship had somehow almost beaten the astropathic messages back to the Imperial capital. The brief communiqué had simply stated that Lansung's efforts at Port Sanctus had been successful. That was all. No casualty figures, no breakdown of what he had actually achieved. Doubtless it was something worthwhile, a genuine victory, otherwise Lansung would not wish to deliver the news in person. Whatever announcement the Lord High Admiral was due to make certainly had the other High Lords excited, except for Veritus. The Inquisitorial Representative had not attended the latest councils to discuss the news and arrange the celebrations and honours about to commence; Vangorich envied him the luxury of choice.

For all that good news from the war was welcome, the ongoing mood of the Senatorum was one of trepidation. Lansung's return would lead to confrontation with Veritus, that much was certain. The Inquisition had the spiritual authority; Lansung had the temporal power. Even the Lord Commander and the Ecclesiarch, two of the most powerful men on the Senatorum, knew that they would be forced to choose one side or the other. For the smaller fish in the pond it was as if a shark and a sea serpent were about to start fighting – and nobody wanted to be swallowed by mistake.

Lansung's procession had reached the Praetorian Way. The armsmen and Lucifer Blacks fell in behind the cortége while the musical accolades continued. Vangorich noted with a sneer that 'Hail the Saviour' was being played; a massive aggrandisement, as the last time that piece had been played had been for the first Lord Commander, Roboute Guilliman.

The parade continued until the echoes of the last rolling drum beats and uplifting chords faded between the Palace towers. At that moment, precisely choreographed, Lansung's skimcar came alongside the steps to the temporary podium that had been erected a hundred feet from the entrance to the Senatorum buildings. The whistling of the wind and the snap of banners were the only sound in the still that followed, everybody's attention on the bulky figure that heaved out of the hovering transport. With surprising nimbleness – shipboard life had shaved off some excess weight – Lansung ascended the steps while his honour guard formed alternating ranks in front of the dais.

'It is with great pleasure and immense pride that I address you today,' began Lansung. His voice emanated from dozens of vox-casters placed along the Praetorian Way and within the gatehouse. 'Honoured troops, lords and ladies of the Senatorum, I bring news that will be welcomed across the Imperium. The ork menace, the darkness that has in recent months plagued our worlds and people, can be defeated!'

There was a rousing cheer from the Lucifer Blacks and armsmen. The High Lords remained silent. A simple bit of rhetoric left them needing more convincing. It seemed as though Lansung was addressing the troops in front of him more than the High Lords, and it was now that Vangorich saw what the Lord High Admiral was doing. He was deliberately placing the Senatorum to the side, his message intended for regimental commanders, fleet admirals and other high officers. He was talking directly to the masses of the Imperial Guard and Navy, not as a High Lord – an inefficient, privileged bureaucrat – but as one of them, a fighting man risking his life for the Emperor and the Imperium.

Manoeuvring Lansung back to the fleet had lessened his power in the Senatorum, but had unwittingly increased his standing with the armed forces he wished to control.

'This very day I bring news of a great victory won by the ships of the Imperial Navy.' By some contrivance a flight of Naval craft chose this moment to perform a fly-past, screeching overhead not far from the gathering. Well-positioned Navy political officers with vid-capture teams were able to track the progress of the aircraft behind Lansung on his podium, an image that would soon find its way far beyond the confines of Terra. Lansung hooked his thumbs into his belt, causing the hanger of his sword to sway a little as he rocked back on his heels. 'At Port Sanctus, an Imperial fleet led by myself and others of the Naval High

Command bested a far more numerous flotilla of ork vessels and improvised installations cordoning the shipyards in that system. Not only was the strength of the ork fleet broken, but the bane of many worlds, that foe which even the great and noble Adeptus Astartes could not overcome, was finally defeated. Yes, brave citizens of the Imperium, your Navy has destroyed one of the so-called ork attack moons.'

Even amongst the disciplined ranks of the Lucifer Blacks this caused a few heads to bob or turn in surprise. Amongst the High Lords, murmuring chatter broke out immediately. Vangorich heard a growl from Veritus. The inquisitor stepped out from the other Senatorum members and started marching towards the dais.

Lansung did not appear worried. He had obviously received word of the changes occurring on Terra whilst en route back to the capital and it seemed to Vangorich that the admiral thought he might handle Veritus as he had Wienand. Vangorich allowed himself an inward smile at the thought of the rude awakening Lansung was about to receive if he thought he could deal and double-deal with the Inquisition now.

'It is true,' continued the admiral. 'By force of arms, by bravery, by skill and by good command, these ork abominations can be defeated. If one can be destroyed, so can they all! The road ahead may be long, it may be dangerous and there may yet be setbacks, but I can say with all surety that the path to victory lies before us and it has been laid by the ships and crews of the Imperial Navy.'

Veritus was at the bottom of the steps by this point, but Lansung was ignoring him, his speech in full stride.

'It is without a moment of hesitation, a gram of reserve, that I can give full assurance to those benighted citizens living under the yoke of ork tyranny, and those of the Emperor's loyal subjects who yet live under the dark fear of the coming greenskin menace, that salvation is coming. By my own hand have I struck a grievous blow to the enemy, and shall do so again at the soonest opportunity. I ask now for the support of the Emperor and his servants. To those that fight in the Imperial Guard, lend me your strength. To those that serve in the Imperial Navy, grant me your bravery. To those that toil in the manufactorums, on the agri-worlds and on the ship-fitting stations, give me your resolve. Between us th–'

Veritus had started to ascend the steps. Rather than the fury Vangorich expected to see on the inquisitor's face, which had seemed to be his permanent expression whilst with the other High Lords, Veritus appeared solemn. Lansung glanced down at the approaching man and there was a look of recognition between them.

Recognition, not surprise. Damn, thought Vangorich, the two of them are in league. But it was not the arrival of his ally that caused Lansung to stop mid-speech.

The world lurched.

Vangorich kept his feet, but others close at hand fell to their knees or backsides. Pieces of masonry and a cloud of dust showered down onto the Praetorian Way from the spires and towers looming around the road. Veritus toppled backwards, the wooden steps splintering under the weight of his armour as he pitched with flailing arms towards the ground. Lansung held on desperately to the rail of the stage, flapping with his free arm.

In the pit of his stomach, Vangorich felt the next shock-wave. It was like nothing he had encountered before. It was, for a brief moment, like being torn inside out, though without any obvious sense of pain.

Dizziness. Dislocation. Disorientation.

Just in front of Vangorich, Mesring was on his hands and knees, vomiting copiously. Others were staggering back and forth, clutching hands to their heads or guts. The Lucifer Blacks and armsmen were scattered across the Praetorian Way like matchwood as the whole road bucked and ripped under their feet.

Dull rumbling reverberated through the ground and walls. Alarms screamed and wailed inside the palaces. Adjutants and aides were squinting and grimacing as they held hands up to the comm-beads in their ears or stooped over vid-receivers.

Vangorich needed no one else to tell him what was happening. He'd read the reports, studying them in excruciating detail while other High Lords had been content to digest the précis. As he felt reality twist again, he stumbled out of the shadow of the massive vaulted Palace gate tower and looked up into the skies. Around him, others were starting to do the same.

He turned, looking from horizon to horizon. The day sky was alight with shooting stars. Streaks of white and silver fell as orbital stations and satellites plunged down Terra's gravity well and were set afire by the atmosphere. Craning his neck, Vangorich looked directly up, into the patch of blue surrounded by the spires of the Imperial Palace. Something glinted above, bigger than anything else that had been in orbit. The sky had turned purple and green around it.

Many miles above, uncaring of Lansung's victory, his speeches or any of the petty politics that had allowed its arrival, a monstrous star fortress larger than anything previously recorded extruded itself into orbit.

The Grand Master of the Officio Assassinorum had never known fear. At that moment, as he watched a false moon rip its way into existence above the Imperial capital, he felt a cold trickle of dread.

ABOUT THE AUTHOR

Gav Thorpe is the author of the Horus Heresy novel *Deliverance Lost*, as well as the novellas *Corax: Soulforge*, *Ravenlord* and *The Lion*, which formed part of the *New York Times* bestselling collection *The Primarchs*. He is particularly well-known for his Dark Angels stories, including the *Legacy of Caliban* series. His Warhammer 40,000 repertoire further includes the Path of the Eldar series, the Horus Heresy audio dramas *Raven's Flight*, *Honour to the Dead* and *Raptor*, and a multiplicity of short stories. For Warhammer, Gav has penned the End Times novel *The Curse of Khaine*, the Time of Legends trilogy, *The Sundering*, and much more besides. He lives and works in Nottingham.

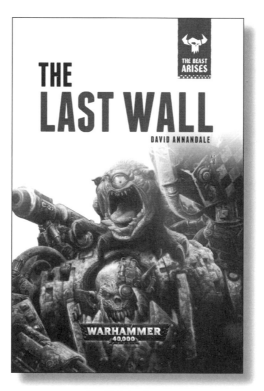